2 Perfect

Sam E. Kraemer

Kaye Klub Publishing

Copyright

♥

This book is an original work of fiction. Names, characters, places, incidents, and events are either the product of the author's imagination or used fictitiously. Any resemblance to actual persons, living or dead, business establishments, events, or locales is entirely coincidental.

Published by Kaye Klub Publishing 2023, 2025

Formatting by TL Travis

Cover by TL Travis

Their story:

♥

Zachary Foxx McMurray and Angus McMurray are happily married and enjoying their life in the small town of Scotland... South Dakota.

Since their wedding at Niagara Falls, Zac has taken up freelance editing and proofreading, having left the bustling world of publishing in New York when he moved to the Midwestern plains to be with his soul mate. The work he's doing isn't fulfilling, but there's a passion project he wants to tackle—turning Gus' numerous short stories into a series of books for children on the autism spectrum.

Angus is still making cabinets and carving statues from wood, but there's something very important to him that he believes would make their lives perfect—a family. Gus hasn't had the courage to broach the subject with Zac, but suddenly, an opportunity arises that makes it his primary focus.

Take the journey with Zac and Gus as they try to achieve their goals while weathering the highs and lows along the way, all the while remembering the reason they were drawn to each other in the first place. With a lot of love, patience, and understanding, can they make their perfect life 2perfect?

Prologue

Zachary Foxx McMurray

"What are you doing?" I asked my husband as I stepped out of the house and onto the front porch.

Angus, or Gus as I called him, had backed his 1975 Ford F-250 pickup into the front yard of our little piece of paradise in Scotland... South Dakota... and stepped down from the driver's side, walking behind the vehicle to lower the tailgate.

"I wanted to move this carving here in the yard, and then I'm taking that bench over to the motel for Mom to put in the lobby. I want to take that table out of there because she hides things in the drawer," he insisted, which made me chuckle.

It was an ongoing battle between my wonderful mother-in-law, Monica McMurray Black Feather, and her only son, Angus McMurray, who happened to be my universe.

Gus didn't want her to smoke because she was a breast-cancer survivor, and Monica had insisted that cigarettes helped with her stress. Martin, her husband, and I stayed as far away from those arguments as we could get. Neither of us wanted to be in the doghouse with our spouses, so we found other things to do when they started antagonizing each other over just about anything.

Just then, Curious George, our calico rescue cat, came slinking up the front steps and wound his way through my legs, the nosy feline. He was nowhere to be found when it was time to go to the vet, but when we were outside, he had to know where we were or what we were doing, thus his name.

George had showed up at the farm late one night, I assumed after having been dumped out by someone who didn't want him. I'd fed the poor kitty because I could see his ribs, and it made me sad. Early the next morning, I called a no-kill shelter in Sioux Falls to see if they'd take him, and they said yes. I made an appointment to take him in the next morning, but the damn cat was nowhere to be found.

Later that evening, I saw Gus walking back from his workshop with the feline in his arms. "Where was he? I was supposed to take him to the—"

Gus cut me off. "He wants to be here, and he can live in the shop. He made himself a nice bed in an old wooden box in there, and he likes it a lot. I took a bowl out there for some water for him, and George will be just fine." That had been the end of the discussion as far as Gus had been concerned.

Gus' insistence that George wanted us always reminded me of our honeymoon in Niagara Falls. We spent three days straight in bed so Gus could ensure I knew how much he wanted me. His endless reassurances were precious to me.

I reached down to pick up George and carried him down the stairs to see what my hunky woodsman was putting in the yard now. The first time I'd watched him move all of those sculptures out of the grass and onto the sidewalk so he could cut the yard, I'd been in awe.

I'd tried to lift one to help him, but he'd patted my ass and leaned forward, whispering, "I'll do the heavy-lifting since Luke doesn't live here, sweetheart. Now and always."

The Luke to whom he was referring was my good friend from college, Jean-Luc Ladeaux, who had been with me on that fateful trip to Scotland where I met the love of my life. I had been there trying to entice Gus to sell his beautiful short-story collection to the publishing house where I worked back then, Pollard & Prentiss Publishing. Then and now, Gus knew how to take my breath away.

I looked down at the piece he was placing on the grass under the eaves of the house to see it was the book he'd been carving when he'd asked me to stay in Scotland the previous June. He hadn't let me see it again, but based on what I was looking at, he'd finally finished it.

The sculpture was carved from an oak stump. There were two perfect replicas of our wedding rings in the seam, and our names were carved at the top, along with our wedding date, June 10, 2021. "It's beautiful, Gus. What is it?" I asked, feeling like a dope because I wasn't sure what it was supposed to represent.

Was it indicative that our life was an open book, and we'd only begun to write our story? That was quite a romantic notion, though in some poetic fashion, Gus seemed to make ordinary gestures into the most loving acts in the world. Of course, that was *this* man's opinion, but I would stand by it.

Gus looked at me and chuckled before his enticing mouth settled into a cute smirk. "It'll be our family album like the ones Mom has, except without the pictures. It's where I'll record all the big things that happen in our lives, and it'll always be there for people to see what a great life we had when we're old and dead," he informed me, once again causing my breath to hitch in my chest. I couldn't hold the chuckle at his bluntness. Gus never really left anything to interpretation. He said *exactly* what he meant.

I knew the man had an idea for the book on the stump, even if I couldn't see it yet. In the year since we'd been married, I'd learned without a doubt that Gus always had a plan. Others might not understand it at first glance, but that was where my faith in him came in. Things always worked out in the end.

"Okay, uh, give me an example of what you'd record on the book aside from our wedding date," I suggested.

"Like when we start our family," he responded, as nonchalant as you please. I stopped breathing.

"Start our *what*?"

Contents

Chapter One

♥

Angus McMurray

I pulled into the parking lot at End of the Trail, my mother's motel, ready to replace that table where she hid her cigarettes. I was done with that business, and she knew it was coming, so she only had herself to blame.

Mom walked out of the office and stood in front of the entrance with her hands on her hips like she always did when she knew she was going to disagree with something I was planning to do. I was used to it by now.

Martin was inside sipping coffee from a motel mug, and he waved at me with a big grin on his face. Martin knew I was there for a reason, and he was smart enough not to come out and get involved in the argument we were about to have. That was how we all got along best.

Zac had *also* decided to stay out of the way, and I appreciated it. This was something my mother and I needed to hash out, just the two of us.

"Angus, son, you're not taking my table," Mom told me, obviously having already received a call from Zac about it. She looked pretty mad, and I wanted to laugh at her, but I didn't want to hurt her feelings.

Monica Black Feather had been the person who loved me and took me home with her when I was ten. She needed to understand my feelings because I hated to fight with her, but I wasn't a kid anymore.

As I stared at her, I stood beside the truck and crossed my arms. "I made the table. I'm taking it with me, but I brought you something else that's nicer," I told her, standing up to her as I was sure she expected.

Mom walked off the porch to see the bench I'd made, and she smiled and nodded. "It's exquisite, Angus, but I like the table."

My mind ran a million miles an hour, trying to land on an explanation she'd accept for why I wanted to take the table away. Maybe we could skip the fight altogether?

Finally, I had a response. "I need to sell the table, Mom. This bench is much better."

I glanced through the window behind her to see Martin watching us closely before he grinned. I waved him out, but he shook his head. He wasn't coming out, which was probably smart.

"I call bullshit, but anyway. I need you to meet someone," Mom told me as if we were done with the conversation. We were far from done, but I'd get back to it.

She tried to help me unload the seat, which was silly because it weighed as much as her. "I've got it, Mom. Just open the door. This will smell much better in here, too," I ordered as I lifted the large cedar bench from the back of my truck and carried it up to the porch, setting it down.

Mom opened the door to the small lobby of the motel, and I stepped inside. "Good morning, Martin. Can I have the table?" I asked as I handed him his coffee cup. He nodded and stood, taking his newspaper and chair with him out of my way.

I moved the table out, opening the drawer there and pulling out the ashtray and the pack of cigarettes to hand to my mother. Her angry face made me chuckle as I carried the table out and put it on the truck, closing the tailgate.

Grabbing the new bench, I carried it inside and put it in the table's spot, moving the chairs to the ends so people could talk if they sat down there. I stepped back and checked it, adjusting the chairs a few times before I was happy with the placement.

"Have a seat, Martin. Doesn't that look nice? Oh, and the cedar smell is much nicer than that nasty smoke. I'll make sure it gets a fresh coat of clear sealer every year," I said before I got ready to leave.

Mom wasn't one to be swayed by my opinion, though I knew without a doubt that she loved me more than anything. I felt the same about her, which was why I wanted her to stop smoking.

"It's a beautiful bench, Angus, but I want my table back. You can't guilt me into doing what *you* want when it goes against what *I* want," she complained.

Taking a deep breath, I knew what I had to say because I'd thought about it. Plus, I'd had a quick discussion with Zac about it before I left the farm, so I was prepared. "I love you. I want you around for a long time. Are you in a hurry to leave me? You love Martin. Are you ready to leave him behind, too?" I asked her as I pointed to her husband and then to her secret cigarettes she was still holding in her hand.

Having already beat breast cancer once, I didn't like the idea Mom would risk having it come back, and if she kept smoking, the chances were high that it would. I'd read it in a medical journal article on Zac's computer.

Mom shoved the wrinkled pack into the pocket of her jeans, as if I'd forget about them if I didn't see them. "No. I'm not ready to leave any of you behind, Angus, but whether or not I smoke isn't your decision to make, son." Then, we had a staring contest like I had with Zac when one of us was trying to make a point.

Finally, she looked away. "Anyway, I want you to meet someone. You've heard Martin mention his friend, Melvin Standing Bear, right? Well, he's taking care of his grandson, and I think you and the boy might become friends, which he needs. His name is Dakota, he's eight, and he's *perfect,* like you. Melvin and Martin are going fishing this weekend, and I'll have Dakota with me, but I thought maybe you and Zachary could come over to help me entertain him. What do you say?" Mom asked me.

It was a simple request, and even though I didn't like new people much, a little boy couldn't be too tough to handle, could he? Zac and I didn't have plans that he'd told me about yet, so I held out my hand and offered my mother my best smile. "We'll come over if you quit smoking," I told her.

I could see Martin smiling and giving me a thumbs up behind Mom where she couldn't see him. I knew he agreed with me.

For a second, I thought she was going to yell at me, but finally, her face softened and she walked over to me, pulling the cigarettes from her pocket and putting them in my hand. "You win. You always win," Mom complained a little.

I wrapped her in my arms. "We both win," I whispered as I hugged her. It was the truth.

The week was routine, just as I liked it to be. Zac was working as a freelance editor through a website, and he was very busy. I'd been installing new cabinets I'd made for the Morrisons' home, which would have been easier if Zac was there to help me, but I wouldn't ask him not to do his work to help me do mine. That wouldn't be fair. It would be as though I thought my job was more important than his, and it wasn't. We were equal partners in our marriage, so I made do.

Thankfully, Mr. Morrison could help me a little—he was a disabled veteran and, in a wheelchair, but he was strong and could help me lift the cabinets to balance on a temporary stand I'd made until I attached them to the wall. It all worked out well enough. I'd thanked him for his help, and he'd smiled.

After a couple of hours, Mr. Morrison spun his chair toward the doorway at the sound of someone walking through the house. "Hey, Mr. Morrison. Your wife let me in."

I turned to see my husband standing in the kitchen doorway, admiring all my work. Mr. Morrison and I had been working so hard, I hadn't realized we were nearly finished. Zac was carrying a paper sack.

"Hello there, Zac. How've you been?" Mr. Morrison politely asked.

"I'm great, Mr. Morrison. I rode my bike over to bring Gus his lunch that he had left on the counter this morning," Zac explained. I'd looked in the bag before I left, and I didn't want what he'd made for me. Tofu salad wasn't good, regardless of where he got the recipe.

"Gotcha. I'm gonna go see if the missus wants to go to Highlander for lunch. Just close up when you finish if

I'm not back, Angus. I'll drop off the check tomorrow if you'll leave me a note with the total," Mr. Morrison said.

I nodded.

Once he and his wife were gone, Zac sat down on a stool and watched me. "So, you didn't like my tofu salad?" he asked me.

I turned my back to him and tried to think of a good lie, but I remembered something my mom had told me when I was younger. "If you say you like it, you'll be eating it once a week." Back then, it was her zucchini soup, and it had no flavor at all.

I hadn't wanted to hurt her feelings, so I said it was good. She was right—I had to eat it once a week for an entire month because she'd frozen single servings I could heat by myself if she was running late getting home from work. Finally, I told her the truth, and she quit making it. It was time to come clean with Zac.

"I'm sorry, but there's something about it I don't like," I admitted, hoping he didn't get upset.

He tried to find vegetarian recipes that I liked to keep things from being boring. I'd told him I was fine eating the same meals all the time because I didn't mind boring, but he wanted to find some new dishes I liked so he could make them for me. He said it wasn't fair that I did all the cooking for us, and he wanted to help.

Cooking all the time didn't matter to me. I loved that he'd sit and talk to me in the kitchen while I made dinner, sometimes helping—which made it take longer—sometimes just telling me about the stories he was editing. Spending time like that was as much fun for me as anything else we did—well, almost anything else. Making love to Zac was still my favorite thing.

"Do you think it was the spice blend I used? It had more of an Ethiopian flare with a berbere mix. Maybe you don't like that palate? I can substitute something else if you tell me what you don't like about it," Zac suggested. He wanted to make it the way I liked it, and I would never like it.

I put down my rechargeable screwdriver and walked over to where Zac was sitting, putting my hands on his shoulders after wiping them on my jeans. I leaned forward and kissed his nose. "I don't like tofu, but I love you."

I let myself get carried away, kissing and hugging on my husband. He was truly my definition of perfection, and when I told him so, his pretty face turned pink, which I loved.

Zac gently pushed me away, reaching for the bag he'd set on the floor. "How much longer will you be?" he asked as he held out the bag to me. When I opened it, delicious smells filled my nose from inside.

I glanced around the room to see I had two more sets of cabinets to put up, but now Mr. Morrison was gone, so it would take me longer. "Probably a couple of hours," I answered as I reached into the bag, pulling out a black bean burger from the diner in town.

After unwrapping it, I took a huge bite, closing my eyes to enjoy the flavor. Once I swallowed, Zac held out a cup of lemonade, giving me a cute smile.

"How about tonight we sit down and make a list of things you like so I can make you a lunch you'll eat and you don't have to lie to me about liking the lunches I make you? I know you don't want to lie, which is something I love very much about you. I don't want you to feel guilty for not admitting something to me, so let's agree to always tell each other the truth and forgive the other if it's something that might sting a little. Together, you know, we can do anything, Gus," Zac told me, touching my face in a reassuring manner.

I nodded and took another bite of my sandwich. Zac sat with me and talked about a book he was working on while I ate, and then when I finished, he stood from the stool and walked over to the cabinets. "Let's get these finished, put my bike in the back of the truck, and go home. I thought maybe we could get the air mattress out, blow it up, and make love under the stars before it gets way too cold to do it anymore. I'll even build a fire in the copper pit, and we can have s'mores," he suggested.

My wrinkled nose made him giggle. "What?"

"Can we get regular marshmallows at the store on the way home? I don't like the vegan ones we had last time."

He nodded, and the two of us got to work.

As we were hanging the last cabinet, I remembered what Mom had told me earlier. "Oh, Mom wants us to come over to the house this Saturday. Martin and Mr. Standing Bear, his friend, are going fishing, and she's entertaining his grandson, Dakota. She says he's like me, and she wants us to meet," I told Zac.

"Like you how?" he asked as he held up the small cabinet on his shoulders while I quickly fastened it to the wall.

"I don't know. Mom didn't say more," I answered honestly. Zac's brow had those wrinkles like he was worried.

"Mom's gonna be there, too. He's a kid. We can't break him," I reminded, hoping to ease his concerns.

Zac chuckled as he shook his head. Once we finished for the day, we swept up the kitchen and left the invoice on the counter, just like Mr. Morrison had asked. I gave him the military discount—fifty percent off the regular price, which I had no problem doing because he'd fought for our country. Zac gave me a sweet kiss before we left and went home.

It was a nice evening—a little cool outside, but with a nice fire and a blanket on the air mattress, Zac and I made love under the stars just like he'd promised. I was happy to make love anywhere, but being outside was the best. The s'mores we shared after were just a bonus.

Chapter Two

Zac

I'd been working on a sapphic romance manuscript for a new client, and I wanted to do my best. I also hoped the two women in the book figured out their shit before the end.

One of the main characters was a masculine-presenting lesbian who owned a plant nursery, and the other was an attorney pondering her plot in life after losing a close friend in a plane crash. *Note-to-self: Don't get on a plane any time soon.*

Victoria, or Vic the botanist as she preferred, was living her life alone but happy, running a large nursery in what seemed to be total contentment. One day, Lana, the lawyer, stumbled in during a rainstorm and Vic was blown away by a pretty redhead, thus the beginning of the turmoil.

It had a lot of fantastic plot points the writer could explore and expand upon in further books, and when she'd approached me to edit the book, she told me she was planning a series. I was looking forward to the additional parts of their story, but for my particular literary tastes, some of the pushing away and pulling back in of the developing relationship bordered on tedious.

Of course, I hadn't been hired to help the writer flesh out the more interesting aspects of the story—I was there to ensure all the commas were in the right place. Proofreading wasn't my favorite thing to do, but it was a paying job and allowed me to live the fairytale existence I enjoyed with Gus.

The back door swung open, and Gus stomped inside. He was wearing a gray beanie on his head, which was unusual. My woodsman ran hot all the time, as the sleeveless flannel shirt he was wearing confirmed. It wasn't like him to get cold and put on a hat, so I had to worry if maybe he was coming down with something.

"You okay?" I asked as I got up from my chair and walked over to the sink where he was washing his hands. I reached up and touched his forehead, relieved he wasn't feverish.

Gus glanced at me and a big smile spread across his face. "You like it?" He turned and tilted his head at different angles, obviously drawing my attention to the gray wool hat he was wearing. As I looked at it, I noticed it was rolled in a manner that didn't cover anything more than the crown of his head.

"It's a hat," I answered, unsure of what he was trying to get me to see.

It was then I realized what was missing—his beautiful long hair wasn't tucked up beneath the hat—it was completely gone. "*Angus! What did you do?*" I gasped, trying not to freak either of us out.

"I saw you looking at that guy in the magazine at the grocery store, the lumberjack-looking guy from that television show. You were smiling at his picture, so I thought you liked how he looked, and I wanted you to smile at me like that."

I'd made the mistake of picking up a gossip rag while waiting in the checkout line. On the cover was this hot bear of a guy who was to be the star of a new gay dating show called *Project Bear Trap.*

The object of the show was typical—ten guys of various gay sub-cultures were trying to win the heart of the bear, who was a damn good-looking man. However, I'd been smiling at the cat in his arms because he looked like our cat, Curious George. In fact, the picture reminded me of Gus and George.

I took a deep breath to calm myself. Gus wasn't Sampson, who lost his strength when Delilah cut off his hair. He was my husband, and he was still quite handsome. I should have been more attentive to his perception of my actions because he was impetuous. He picked up on the subtlest nuances that most others would completely ignore.

"One, I wasn't looking at the guy. You're much more handsome than any man I've ever met, and I'll remind you that you made these rings for us."

I held up my hand to point at my wedding ring before pointing at his. "We have a legal agreement that will be very costly and time consuming for you to get out of. Besides, I was looking at the cat in his arms and thinking how much it looked like George."

At hearing his name, the cat came slinking through the porch door that was still ajar and into the kitchen. He wound through Gus' legs until Gus reached down and picked him up, holding George exactly the way the guy had on the magazine cover.

"Two, I hope you see me smile at you like that all the time. Don't ever change anything about yourself just because you think I'd like it. I love you exactly how you are. That's the reason I fell in love with you in the beginning. You are wonderfully unique," I confirmed for him by placing my hand over his heart.

Gus mindlessly ran his right hand over George's head, making the lazy cat purr like a motorcycle. "I love you exactly how you are, too. This made me look more like a dad, though. I told Ray exactly how to cut it, and he did a good job, right?"

I plucked the hat from the top of his head and circled him to see it was a great cut, but oh, how I'd miss his beautiful long hair. I stepped back and noticed he looked a little older than he had... more distinguished, if that made any sense.

"Where'd you get the hat? Why'd you get a hat?" I asked him.

He put George down and stepped closer to me. "I thought you liked hats. I look more grown-up now. Ray even said so."

Ray Miller was the town barber who usually did a terrible job cutting hair, if most of the men walking around Scotland, South Dakota, with terribly tragic haircuts were any sign.

"How'd you tell him to cut it?" I asked, noticing the proud smile on Gus' face.

"I went to the store and bought the magazine, and I told him to do it exactly like the man on the cover. I made him give me a mirror so I could see what he was doing, and I told him when it wasn't right," Gus stated, puffing up his chest a bit.

Did that bitchy old man seriously take instructions from my husband? I wished to hell I'd have been there to witness that exchange.

"Did he get upset because you were giving him instructions?" I further inquired.

"He's afraid of me. Mom told me so." Gus leaned forward and kissed my nose, but his comment troubled me.

"Why's he afraid of you?" I asked, feeling anger burn in my gut. I'd go to that fucking barber shop and give him a sizeable chunk of my mind for being a judgmental asshole before I sliced off an ear with the man's own straight razor if it was because of Gus' Asperger's.

"After Mom adopted me, she took me straight to the barber shop for a haircut because at the group home where I lived, we all got bowl haircuts. I was ten back then, and I had a meltdown because Ray kept yelling at me to sit still and pinching my shoulder. I'd never go back there after that, so Mom said I could let it grow. She trimmed my hair at home if it needed it. When I went in there this morning, he looked really scared to see me and cut it exactly how I told him I wanted," Gus explained, which made me laugh until tears were leaking from my eyes.

Gus laughed with me, holding me against his powerful chest, and I was suddenly in the mood for more than a quick cuddle. "Come with me, woodsman," I teased as I took his hand and led him to the bedroom.

"Are we going to have sex because I got my hair cut?" He tilted his head in such a cute way, I couldn't help myself.

I smirked at him. "Do you really care why?"

Gus released that deep laugh I loved before he picked me up. "Nope, not really."

He took me into the bedroom and gently placed me on the bed before he stood and stripped off his sleeveless flannel shirt, showing me his beautiful, muscular torso. Thankfully, he hadn't touched the sexy curls between his pecs where I loved to brush my nose while he plowed me into the mattress.

The man reeked of masculinity, and I was like a glue-sniffing deviant when he was near. I reached for his jeans and flipped the brass button open, lowering the zipper as the sound echoed in the quiet room.

"Can I kiss you here?" I teased by pulling down the band of his boxers to see the dark head of his hard cock. I touched the slit with my index finger to pick up the pre-come waiting for me.

"Oh, god yeah," he gasped as I jerked his jeans and underwear down at the same time. They pooled at his ankles as I licked up his length, drowning in his scent.

"*Fuck!!*" Gus groaned as I took him inside my mouth, sucking him down to the root. I pulled back and did it again, feeling his hands rest on my head. He didn't grip me, just carded his fingers through the strands and let me control the speed and depth of how far I took him.

I brushed my fingers up the outside of his thighs, to his hips, and over his hard abdomen before I pulled back and swirled my tongue around the head of his dick. He thrust shallowly before pulling out of my mouth.

"Inside you, please," he whispered as he worked to get his boots off, nearly falling onto the floor on his ass as he did. He finally slowed down and sat on the bed next to me, taking the time to unlace the old brown steel toe boots and set them out of the way. He then took off socks, pants, and boxers before he looked at me, his sexy smile sending a zing to my leaking dick.

"Clothes off or I'll take them off, and you don't like that," Gus stated firmly.

That was no shit. Since I'd married Gus, I'd lost more jeans, shirts, and frilly panties than I could count. Of course, after Gus destroyed them, he always ordered new ones to replace them. Unfortunately, they always had to go back because they weren't exactly my style—except for the panties. He was a dirty, dirty boy with a new fetish...

The jeans I was wearing were some of my favorites, so I hurried to remove them, along with my sweatshirt, leaving me in powder blue silk panties that matched the blue polish on my toes.

"Beautiful," Gus whispered as he climbed on the bed and reached for the lube on the nightstand. We'd ditched the condoms after our second round of tests—Gus wanted to be sure he had nothing that could bring me harm, so he'd insisted we get tested twice within the first six months of our marriage.

I'd worked very hard not to get frustrated with the extra waiting time. In my heart, I knew the man loved me and was only looking out for my well-being.

After quick prep, Gus slid home inside me, and as always, he waited for me to tell him I was okay for him to continue. I nodded, and he exhaled. "I love you, Zac," he whispered as he moved inside me.

My woodsman was quite a cocksman, but he always started out slow and gentle. I relished his tender loving care, and this time was no different. He leaned down, but there was no long hair curtained around us. I missed that.

"I love you, too, Gus. Oh, damn," I moaned as he hit the sweet spot with a hard thrust. My eyes nearly did a three-sixty in their sockets.

He continued his steady pace, driving me out of my mind. I felt more loved in that moment than anyone ever had, I was sure. "Baby, can you go faster?" I pleaded.

With a teasing wink, that man revved my motor to its peak. "Sweetheart, I can't wait. Are you..." His voice was breathy and definitely did the trick.

Before I could answer him, I erupted between us from just the friction of his abs and happy trail. Suddenly, Gus sucked in a breath, and I felt the warmth of his release inside me. "Oh, fuck yeah," he added before he collapsed, his head resting on my chest in exhaustion.

I ran my fingers through his shorter mane, feeling the softness I was so familiar with. The short hairs at the back of his neck were tickly as I stroked them, and when Gus laughed as he slipped from my body, I laughed, too.

"I like the haircut, by the way. You left it longer on the top, and I like it. I can't believe it's possible, but it makes you even more handsome," I told him as he rolled off me and pulled me with him.

I snuggled into my favorite place in his arms and exhaled. It was as close to heaven as I'd likely ever get.

Something came to mind while we rested there together, and I felt like it was time to explore it. "Gus, those stories you've written... Have you thought about publishing them?"

"Did your crazy boss from New York call and ask for them?" Gus asked.

I hadn't heard from anyone at Pollard & Prentiss Publishing since I'd walked out of their office that day and Joy, Penelope Prentiss' assistant, had wished me well. I still believed Gus' stories would be a perfect children's series. The way he told them showed that he'd put a lot of himself into them, and I believed they were beautiful and needed to be shared.

"No, no. I just think there are kids out there who might enjoy your stories. We could find an illustrator and turn them into children's books with colorful drawings, or we could do one large storybook. I just want you to think about it, okay?" I suggested.

Angus was quiet, so I lifted my head to see he was sound asleep. I returned to my favorite place on his firm body—his shoulder—and joined him in dreamland.

Chapter Three

Gus

Saturday morning, I was in the wood shop sanding a small wooden truck to offer to Dakota. It was the third vehicle I'd made over the week between other projects, and I hoped he liked them. I planned to stop at the supercenter outside of town on the way to Mom's so I could pick up some paints for Dakota to paint them if he wanted.

Mom and I used to love to paint pictures together. Before she married Martin, they were taped all over the house. When we moved, she put them in frames and hung them in my room at the house we shared with Martin, and to this day, they were still hanging in my old bedroom.

I hoped the boy liked the toys. I didn't know anything about him or if I'd like him at all, but Mom had said he was perfect, and I trusted her.

Once I'd attached the wooden wheels I'd carved, I pushed it across the worktable to make sure it rolled. I put it into the cloth grocery bag with the others and walked toward the house. When I opened the back door, I saw Zac at the table, hard at work on his computer.

He looked up at me and smiled, which made me happy in a flash. It was the look he had on his face when he'd seen the guy on the cover of that magazine, and now it was for me, just as I wanted.

"You ready?" he asked me as he closed his laptop.

We'd already had breakfast before I went out to the shop to finish the little truck. I was excited to meet the boy, but I wasn't going to get my hopes up that he'd like us in return. I didn't like everyone I met when I was his age. I still didn't.

Zac grabbed our coats as we went through the mudroom and outside to the truck. He headed to the passenger side, but I grabbed his coat sleeve to steer him the other way. It was time to give him more driving lessons.

"What?" Zac asked as I led him around and opened the driver's side door.

"You need to practice more, and this time don't burn out the clutch," I said, offering him a smile and hoping I didn't sound mad. I wasn't at all. It had been kinda funny when it happened on our honeymoon, but Zac felt terrible about it back then. I didn't want him to still feel bad.

I had a hard time figuring out what people were thinking or how my comments to them made them feel. It was part of me having Asperger's, as the doctor had told my mom when I was first diagnosed a long time ago, and it still bugged me.

Once Zac was in the truck, I closed his door and walked around to the other side, hopping in and sliding over the bench seat to the middle. I put the bag with the cars on the floorboard and shoved the keys in the ignition. "Okay, sweetheart. First, put on your seatbelt," I told him as I fished out the middle belt and put it around my waist. "Next, adjust your mirrors."

Zac turned and stared at me. His face had a funny look I couldn't figure out.

"What's wrong?" I asked.

I took driving lessons seriously. When Mom had taught me, she'd kept squeezing my arm. "Angus, slow down." *Squeeze.* "Angus, see the car stopped at the corner." *Squeeze.* "Oh, god! Watch out for that—" *Squeeze.*

"I know how to drive a car, honey. I just don't know how to drive a *stick shift*," Zac reminded me.

"Okay. Sorry." I put my arm around his shoulders and kissed his cheek, waiting until he was comfortable and had adjusted his mirrors for us to continue with the lesson.

He sat there with his hands on the wheel, staring out the window for a moment. "Why am I driving *this*? Maybe we should get an automatic instead? I'm sure someone would love this truck. It's just not *me*," Zac announced, surprising me. I didn't know he didn't like my truck. I loved it.

I wanted to get mad at him for his comment, but I really couldn't. It was okay if he didn't like it. We didn't have to like everything the same. Plus, I didn't want to stress him out because it's too hard to learn anything when stressed.

"How about we talk about getting another vehicle at another time, okay?" I told him as I kissed his cheek again, trying to direct him back to learning to drive the truck we *had*.

I exhaled to relax, and then something came to mind. "So, what if I got cut in the wood shop and couldn't drive myself to the doctor? What would you do?"

Zac's head turned so fast I thought he was going to hurt his neck. "Why on earth... Why would you put that out into the universe? *Oh my god!* Angus, you've damn near guaranteed that you're going to get hurt and now I'm going to have to sit in the shop with you to make sure you're... *Why would you do that?*" He was getting way too upset, but maybe that was good?

"It's just a possibility it could happen. So, tell me what you would do?" I asked him again.

Zac exhaled. "Okay. I push in the clutch and put my foot on the brake to start the truck," he announced. I nodded, and he did just that.

I'd once bragged to him that I could teach a monkey to drive a stick shift, but I was thinking maybe I was full of crap. Each time he ground the gears, I poked his shoulder hard. I could suddenly understand why Mom squeezed my arm.

When we got back into the truck after stopping at the store for paint, Zac got in on the passenger's side, thankfully. I could smell the burning clutch, and I didn't want to have to get a new one, but I didn't want to hurt his feelings. Then I had an idea—Mom could teach him.

I drove us to Mom and Martin's house, parking at the curb in front. "I'll ask Mom to teach you to drive a stick shift in her car. It might be easier," I commented before I got out. It would also save my truck more damage.

Grabbing the bags from the floorboard, I walked around and opened his door. I offered my hand to Zac, who took it and stepped out before he started rubbing his left shoulder. "What's wrong?" I asked him.

He turned around and started poking me in the chest with his finger really fast and hard. "How's that feel, Angus?" He wasn't smiling, so I had to guess he was mad at me for my pokes when he was grinding the gears while driving.

I gently took his hand in mine, stopping it from pecking at me like a chicken's beak, and lifted it to my lips to give his knuckles a kiss. "I love you."

Zac stared at me for a minute before he shook his head. "That will not work every time, you know." I smiled at him—just glad it worked *this* time.

We went around the house to the back porch to go inside, and we heard Mom humming in the kitchen. "Hello, beautiful," Zac greeted, hugging Mom tight as she hugged him, too. Seeing the two of them together made me feel warm in my chest.

Mom turned to me and raised her right eyebrow, which was something I couldn't do, though over the years I'd tried to learn. "Your hair looks very nice, Angus," Mom told me as she stepped forward to hug me. Her hugs were the best, and I always loved them.

"Thank you, Mom. Where's the kid?" I asked as I looked around the kitchen.

"His name is Dakota, and he's in your room. He's not a fan of loud noises, but he's a very sweet boy. Just go sit down and wait for him to come to you," Mom stated.

I nodded and went to the hallway by the front door to slide off my boots. I had the bag with me that held the toy cars and paints, and I walked upstairs, stopping at the open door of my bedroom.

Everything in the room was the same as it had been in our old house—sky blue walls with white trim; a queen-sized bed with cowboys on the bedspread; and my old television setting on a white chest of drawers. Even the pictures I used to paint that Mom had framed were still on the walls.

I remembered how hard it had been to adjust to the new room with all the unfamiliar sounds in Martin's house. I'd been freaked out those first few nights and didn't sleep at all.

All the noises seemed to blend into a spooky symphony. The traffic on the highway that was about five-hundred yards away made me worry they were going to drive through Martin's house. The creaking floors had me imagining someone was pacing outside my door. A huge pine tree outside my window brushed against the glass when there were gusts of wind. They'd all combined to scare the hell out of me that first week, but the tree had been the worst.

Mom had asked me why I was so grumpy every morning at breakfast, but I was scared to tell her the reason. I was afraid she'd get mad at me for not giving our new home a chance. Afraid she'd think I hadn't been trying to adjust to my new surroundings and her marriage to Martin.

Finally, the third night, Mom had come into my room to talk to me, and she'd heard the tree scraping against the window. She'd quickly gone to get Martin so he could hear it, too.

He'd stood in my room for a couple of seconds before he'd rushed out, which had worried me as much as the tree sounds. Was he leaving us because I complained about his nice house?

Thirty seconds later, Mom and I heard the roar of a chainsaw and the crash of a tree falling away from the window during a thunderstorm. For taking away that horrible sound, I'd always be grateful to Martin.

Mom loved Martin, and based on what he'd done for me that night, I knew he was a kind man. After the tree was gone, it didn't take too long for me to be happy with my new home, too.

I sat on the floor in the doorway of my old room, giving the boy a chance to see me at his level without being frightened. He was wearing black, fuzzy earmuffs, which were a surprise to me, but if they helped him cope with sounds, then I was glad he had them.

I reached into the fabric bag and pulled out one of the little wooden cars I'd made for him, slowly rolling it across the wooden floor to where Dakota was leaning against the end of the bed with a picture book.

When the car bumped his leg, he quickly glanced at it before turning his head to see me sitting on the floor. I didn't say anything to him, just smiling and pulling out another car—a race car style. I rolled it toward him, and he offered a small smile.

Dakota reached for the race car, stopping before he touched it and glancing at me. I nodded, and he picked it up, turning it in his hands for a moment before spinning one wheel.

I reached into the bag again and pulled out the pickup truck, rolling it halfway toward him this time. The boy took in the sight of the little truck I'd made of pine and then glanced at me.

When I nodded, Dakota crawled closer, settling on his knees next to where the truck had stopped. He stared at me for a second before he glanced down at the truck again.

I wondered if he was non-verbal. I'd met kids like that before when I was younger and going to occupational therapy. I knew they didn't want to be that way, but it was hard for them to feel comfortable enough to speak in front of others. Mom had explained it to me so I knew it wasn't because they didn't like me.

I stuck my hand into the bag and pulled out a paint set, holding it out to him. He sat back in his original spot, staring at me before he rolled the first car back to me. I smiled at him. "Hi," I said quietly and waved, too, in case he couldn't hear me through the earmuffs.

He didn't answer, just returning my wave for a second. His eyes met mine, and I felt a jolt in my chest like I'd never felt before. I needed to talk to Zac about it because I wasn't sure if that was normal.

I reached into the bag and pulled out two paint brushes, holding out my empty hand and brushing over it. "You want to paint the cars?" I asked him, my voice in a whisper.

He reached up and took off the earmuffs, looking at me again. "Can you paint?" I asked, keeping my voice quiet. Dakota nodded, and my heart beat a little faster.

"Be right back," I told him as I scooted out of the room on my butt. I remembered being scared of people who were tall, and I didn't want to frighten the boy, so I didn't stand until I was in the hallway.

I went downstairs and walked into the kitchen where Mom and Zac were peeling apples. "What are you making?" I asked them.

"Applesauce. Melvin said Dakota likes it, so I thought I'd make some for him to have with dinner. You'll stay, right?" Mom asked.

She opened the fridge and pointed to fry bread dough and a large bowl of marinating vegetables, and my stomach was on board immediately. Mom made the best fry bread.

"Yep." I then turned to Zac. "You want to come meet him? We're going to paint the cars I made."

"Do you think he's okay to meet me already?" Zac asked. I thought he was worried, but I was terrible at judging other people's reactions.

I stared at Mom, who smiled at Zac. "He'll be fine. Let Gus show you how to approach him. He is a sweet boy—he's just skittish about meeting new people. His mother was a drug addict and used to mistreat him because he was different and she didn't know how to take care of him. If she'd only reached out, things could have been a lot different for both of them."

Mom glanced at me, and I knew why she'd said he was like me. My birth mother did the same to me. I remembered some of it, but I tried not to think about it because it made Mom and me sad.

I went to the bin where Martin put his old newspapers and grabbed some so we didn't get paint everywhere. Mom handed me some paper plates and two plastic cups for water.

"Gus, go on up. I'll send up some drinks and snacks with Zac. It'll just be a minute," she said.

I took everything with me and slowly climbed the stairs, trying to miss the ones that made noises. When I got back to my old room, Dakota was still looking at the little race car in his hands, but he had a smile on his face. That made me happy.

Chapter Four

Zac

Monica and I were peeling apples while Gus went upstairs to talk to the grandson of Martin's friend. "Where're his parents?" I asked her as I used the vegetable peeler she'd given me after I cut my thumb with the knife.

"His mother, Kristi, died of a drug overdose when Dakota was just five. For the last three years, Melvin has been raising him on his own. He and Kristi's mother divorced years ago, and he never remarried." Monica was being a little too cagey about the boy's father for my tastes. There was definitely something she wasn't sharing with the group.

"Wow. That's quite an undertaking for a grandfather. Does the boy go to school?" I asked, eager for more information.

It seemed odd to me that Monica wanted Gus to meet the boy first. Gus had said the boy was perfect, but I had to wonder if it was *her* definition of perfect, as she always referred to my Gus. In my mind and heart, the man *was* perfect, but not in the way Monica used the word.

"He does. Three days a week, Melvin takes him to Sioux Falls for school, and two days a week, he has a tutor come to their home to work with him." That piqued my interest.

"Why doesn't he go to Scotland Elementary?" I asked her, putting down the vegetable peeler and grabbing a towel to wipe my hands.

Monica began humming and chopping the apples into small chunks to put into a sauté pan. She then went to the fridge and grabbed the butter dish, chunking up the stick inside and tossing the pieces into the pan with a pinch of salt before she put on the lid and turned to me.

"Dakota can't attend the elementary school in town because he has autism. The school couldn't help Angus when he was a boy, and they're still not prepared to help children on the spectrum like Dakota," she announced.

Okay...

"He's a little boy with a lot of challenges, Zac, and he's probably about the level Angus was when I got him. You see how far Gus has come, and I'm telling you, Dakota can thrive as well with love and support. You and Gus can do so much for this little boy, but it will take time," Monica stated.

I stood from the stool where I'd been sitting and stared at the woman as if she had two heads. "What?"

Monica went to wash her hands, glancing toward the stairs. "Melvin found out he's got cancer, Zac. For the last six months, Martin has been taking him for treatments, and I've been caring for Dakota, along with a few of the women in town, but Dakota has been regressing. He needs a stable family, and I believe he notices Melvin is deteriorating."

Just then, heavy steps were coming down the stairs, so we stopped talking. Gus came into the kitchen, his face glowing with excitement. There was a quick discussion with Monica about staying for dinner, and then Gus turned to me, his eyes filled with joy. "You want to come meet him? We're going to paint the cars I made."

I quickly glanced at Monica and then turned back to Gus. I was certain my fear was like a neon sign on my face. "Do you think he's okay to meet me already?"

Thankfully, Monica picked up on my concern, though I didn't believe Gus did. She told him to head upstairs with the boy and that I'd be there with snacks.

Once Gus had gathered things for painting and lumbered back upstairs, I turned to Monica, panic overtaking my body. I was having a hard time catching my breath, so she reached into a drawer and grabbed a small paper bag, bringing it around to me and showing me how to hold it over my face.

"Breathe into the bag and listen to me. There's no reason at all to freak out, Zac. Angus was sensitive to sounds and had anxiety, too. He threw tantrums and acted out until I could show him I loved him and I wouldn't let anyone hurt him. You and Zac can be this boy's champions, I just know it," she whispered as she stroked my back.

Finally, my breaths slowed and mirrored hers, and I took the bag away. "I don't know anything about being around babies," I whispered as Monica took the bag from me.

She grabbed a small basket, draping it with a clean towel and putting in some fruit chews, small packs of cheese crackers, and a bowl with some apple slices. "Then it's a wonderful thing that he's a little boy and not a baby, isn't it?" Monica said as she opened the fridge and grabbed some juice boxes and a bottle of sparkling lemonade for me.

"Oh, after what just happened, you think I'm meant to help a little boy with…" I wasn't even sure how to phrase it, but the fear was bone-deep.

I was an insensitive prick. I looked out for number one, and I took no prisoners in my crusade to come out on top. I wasn't the kind of person who was patient and compassionate, who would be empathetic to the needs of a boy who saw the world differently.

"Go up there and just watch them together, Zachary. I'm not asking you to do anything more than watch," Monica said.

I wasn't sure she knew what she was doing, but I nodded and slowly walked upstairs in my socked feet, cringing when the stairs creaked. My anxiety was building with every step.

Outside the door, I heard Gus whispering. "Yeah. You can mix the colors if you want."

The gentleness in his voice had my eyes tearing up as I realized I was getting the rare opportunity to observe my husband—the way he'd been as a child, and how far he'd come.

I dried my eyes on my shirt by lifting my shoulders and stepped into the doorway, seeing a beautiful smile on my husband's face as he watched the little boy with brown hair and tan skin sitting on his feet with his little tongue between his lips. Dakota was painting inside a line Gus had drawn on the wooden toy truck where the windshield would be. It took my breath away.

I tiptoed into the room and put the basket and drinks on the floor by Gus. Like a shot, the little boy scrambled behind the bed and screamed, scaring the shit out of me. I dropped onto the floor in the fetal position, sure we were under siege by pirates or ninjas.

Gus rushed over to me, but I pointed toward the boy, so he scrambled over to the bed at the same time someone came running up the stairs. I felt hands on my back as Monica leaned forward. "Come downstairs with me," she whispered.

I jumped to my feet and ran down the stairs, slowing only to slide on my shoes and dart out the front door. I ran down the street, heading to nowhere at all. As was just confirmed, I was the most ill-equipped person in the world to care for a child, and I felt less than worthless.

I was sitting in a rocking chair on the front porch of End of the Trail, not sure if I should go back to Monica and Martin's house, or if I should call the Used Car King of Scotland, Anders Milton, to see if he would give me a ride out to the farm.

There were no guests at the motel, so I didn't have to worry about anyone bothering me or thinking I was going to rob the place. The police knew me because everyone in town knew my Gus, so I was safe, though it was getting chilly as the sun was going down.

Martin's pickup came to a stop in front of the motel and he lumbered out, carrying my jacket. The guilt that washed over me at making him come looking for me when he was supposed to be fishing with his friend was embarrassing.

I stood. "Hi, Martin. I'm sorry you had to come looking for me. I was deciding if I should walk back or just call Anders Milton to come pick me up and take me home."

Martin chuckled. "Hey, I understand, Zac. I wasn't fishing, anyway. I took Milton to see a lawyer in town to prepare his will. His docs say he needs to get his affairs in order." Martin Black Feather really was a kind man, but a talker... he wasn't.

He sat down in the rocking chair next to me, staring toward the street as we rocked in tandem. After a couple of minutes, I felt a little uncomfortable. I slid on my jacket and turned to Martin. "Should we go?"

He propped his elbow on the arm of the rocker, stroking his chin in thought for a few more minutes, and then he spoke. "I remember when I met Monica. Prettiest woman I'd ever seen, and I could tell in a hot minute she was a force of nature."

I was so surprised by his words, I couldn't speak. My lack of acknowledgement didn't faze him.

"I asked her out about five times when I was at the center where she worked to fix one plumbing emergency or another. The kids were always throwing things down the toilets and clogging them up because they loved to watch them swirl in the bowl."

Martin chuckled, and I joined him. The man had the patience of a saint.

"Anyway, she refused to go out with me every damn time I asked. Then, one day when I showed up to unclog a bathroom drain where someone had pushed little metal cars down to the elbow, I decided, what the hell? I asked her again—by then it was like a joke to me—and I'll be damned if she didn't say I had to meet her son before she'd even think about going out with me. She invited me to her place for a non-date dinner, and I went. God, I bet she told me ten times it wasn't a date."

It was sweet the way he just stared at the darkening sky as though he was visualizing that first non-date.

I chuckled. I'd heard a little of the story before from Monica, but never anything from Martin. All I knew for sure was that the man was head-over-heels in love with her, and he was good to Gus. That was pretty much all I needed to know.

"How was it? Meeting Gus at fifteen?" I asked.

Martin snorted. "Intimidating. Hell, he was almost as big as he is now, and he didn't like me at all. He didn't scream at me like Dakota screamed at you, but he had this stare that scared the piss outta me."

I laughed. I'd seen my husband's glaring stare a time or two when we were dealing with clients at the woodworking shop. My man had a distinct look of displeasure.

"What did you do to win him over?" I asked.

"I cut down a tree. Even at fifteen, a lot of things scared him, and when Monica and I got married so quick and they moved in with me, poor Gus jumped at every noise around the house."

I had a feeling I knew where the story was going, but I let him talk. He rarely did when I was around.

"One night when we were getting ready to go to bed, Monica went to check on him because he'd been really quiet that evening, and he barely touched his dinner. He was freaking out. She heard the tree branches brushing against his window and figured out what was wrong. When she told me what was going on, I got out the chainsaw and cut the damn thing down in the middle of a thunderstorm," Martin explained.

It was such a sweet story. Best thing I'd heard in a long time, and as I thought about it, I realized it would be a perfect story for Gus to write.

"That was all it took?" I asked him.

He nodded. "After that, Gus decided I was okay. He picked up on the fact I wouldn't let anything bad happen to him or his mom, and over time, we developed a relationship. I even taught him how to fix things around the house, and he was a first-rate helper when I had big plumbing jobs."

"Wow. That's so sweet. Did you teach him to carve?"

"No, that was all Gus. He started carving little figures out of wood after Monica learned to trust him with a pocketknife, and he taught himself to do some of the most incredible pieces of art that I've ever seen in my life. The cabinet and furniture making came later. It was a slow process for Gus and me to trust each other, Zac, but over time, we figured it out."

I sat there for a few more seconds, thinking about what he'd said. I really needed to talk to Gus. I hoped to hell I hadn't done any lasting damage to the little boy. The two of them together had been adorable before I ruined everything.

"Martin, would it be terribly rude if you took me home instead of back to your house? I know Dakota is staying for dinner, and I don't want to disrupt things again. Maybe we can try to be friends another time," I said, holding back the tears. I'd cry those at home by myself.

Chapter Five

Gus

My husband had scared Dakota, but he hadn't meant to. Zac had brought up snacks, and he'd come into the room without shoes like Mom must have told him. When the boy had seen him, he'd panicked and scrambled under the bed.

I wasn't sure why, but Zac had rolled into a ball on the floor. Now, I had *two* problems on my hands.

Zac pushed me away when I tried to take care of him, and he'd pointed toward the bed where Dakota had crawled under. I went over there and sat down on the floor nearby to wait for Dakota to come out, remembering how I'd done the same thing more than once. I knew eventually, he'd want to know what was going on in the room, so I waited.

Mom told Zac to come downstairs, and a few seconds later, I heard the front door slam, which probably wasn't good. Mom came back upstairs and stood in the doorway. "Zac took off, but Martin went to find him."

I nodded and sat there for a while, staring at the walls where all my old pictures were hanging. I had an idea that might not be great, but if Zac wanted to make my stories into books for kids, why couldn't Dakota and I draw the pictures?

I could draw the outlines for him. I'd drawn most of them before I wrote the stories, but maybe that would be a thing Dakota would like to do with me?

"I have a story to tell you," I said in a quiet voice because I was pretty sure if he was interested, Dakota would slide closer to hear it after I started.

"When I was about your age, I had a dog named Mike. He was a black and white border collie, and he just showed up on our porch one morning. My mom wanted to send him away because we didn't want a dog, but Mike would run off when she was around and show up when she wasn't. Finally, Martin said he could stay, so I had a friend to keep me company. I didn't like being around many people because I thought they were loud, and I didn't like big noises," I said, telling him about my dog, Mike.

A small hand crept from under the bed, so I handed Dakota his earmuffs in case he needed them. He pushed them away and peeked his head out, resting it on his hand to listen. I kept going.

I told Dakota the story of my best friend and how we were always together before I gave him to a boy like me. He listened carefully when I explained how the two of them became good friends, and how Mike ended up moving away when the boy's parents left town because of the father's job.

By the time I was done, Dakota was sitting next to me with his back against the wall like mine. His head was down, but he was listening as his earmuffs were resting on his left knee. He didn't seem to be scared anymore, which was good.

Mom came upstairs and sat on the bed. "Are you guys hungry? There are vegetable and cheese fry bread sandwiches. I also made some applesauce."

I turned to Mom. "Is Zac still..."

Mom shook her head and left the room. I was anxious about where my husband had gone, but I knew why he'd left. Dakota had been surprised and acted out. Zac didn't understand why, but I could explain it to him when I found him.

"I'm going downstairs to eat. If you're hungry, come down," I said in a soft voice. I got up and walked downstairs, hoping Dakota would come down, too. If not, I knew Mom would bring him a plate upstairs like she'd done for me so many times when I was a kid and couldn't go to the table.

I checked around downstairs once more, just to be sure Zac hadn't come back. When I didn't find him, I walked into the kitchen to see Mom finishing up dinner.

"Where'd he go?" I went to the cabinet to get plates to set the table. It had always been my job as a kid, and I still liked to help.

"Martin took him home. He said Zac was pretty rattled. He believes it's his fault Dakota got upset," Mom told me.

I rolled my eyes, which my mom hated. "That's dumb."

Mom put her hand on her hip and raised her eyebrow again as she leaned against the counter. I could tell she wasn't happy with my answer. "Think about it, Angus. We had those days and nights where you were unhappy when things happened you weren't prepared for, remember?"

I was taken back to a memory of sleeping in the front closet in Mom's apartment the first time I spent the weekend with her before she became my mom. I was afraid to sleep in the room she'd fixed up for me. It was new and scary, so I wouldn't sleep in there by myself after being used to sharing a bigger room with three other boys like me. I didn't want to be that way, but I couldn't help it back then.

Mom was right, so I nodded before I asked, "Should I call him?"

I could hear soft footsteps coming down the stairs. When Dakota stepped on the third step and it made a noise, he stopped. I started to go to the hallway, but Mom snapped her fingers and shook her head, so we waited.

Instead, I went to the drawer to get the utensils, and when Dakota came into the kitchen and stood in the corner, earmuffs on and the little pickup in his hands, I walked over and held out the knives, forks, and spoons. "Can you set the table with me?"

Mom had asked me that question so many times in the beginning, and it always made me feel good to help her because there were so many things I couldn't do. I held out my hands with the silverware, and we walked around the table, Dakota placing utensils at each plate with me explaining where they went and why—just like Mom taught me.

When he put the last spoon on the table, he looked up and smiled. I held up my fist, and he bumped it before I pulled out the chair for him. He was a little short for the table, so Mom went to the living room and came back with a pillow she grabbed. I helped him down and held his hand while she doubled it and put it in the chair with a towel over it in case there was a spill.

I kneeled down and smiled at him. "Can I help you up there?"

He nodded before he took off his earmuffs and handed them to me. I put them on the table next to his plate and picked him up, putting him in the seat and pushing the chair forward so he could reach everything.

I felt guilty about staying to eat while Zac was at home by himself, but I knew in my heart that my husband would understand if I explained everything to him when I got there.

The house was dark when I drove up and parked beside the shop. The flood light that faced the barn was on, so I grabbed the plate Mom had sent home for Zac and headed toward the house.

Dakota was spending the night with Mom while Martin went back to Mr. Standing Bear's house. Martin had called him and found out the man wasn't feeling well, so Mom had thawed some broth for him and sent it with Martin.

I'd told Mom I'd be back in the morning to paint the other cars with Dakota and try to get to know him better. The boy was going to lose his grandpa, which made me sad. I was sure he was feeling like everybody was leaving him behind, and I hated it for him.

After I put the plate of food in the refrigerator, I moved around the house, not seeing Zac anywhere, so I checked the windows and doors to be sure everything was locked up tight before I went to bed.

I'd locked the shop and the barn earlier in the day before we'd gone to Mom's house, so I was sure George was okay with food, water, and heat. It was getting cold out, and I didn't want him left outside, but I wouldn't bring him into the house. He was an outside cat, and I respected his choice to be one.

I went to our bedroom, seeing Zac curled up in the middle of the bed. He was asleep, so I hurried to undress and join him. He jerked awake and looked at me after I crawled in next to him.

"I'm sorry," he whispered. He tried to get away when I pulled him close to me, which made me laugh.

"You're cold. Your feet are like ice," Zac complained, though it wasn't with any anger.

I laughed and held him that much tighter. "I know, and as my husband, it's your job to warm me up. Why are you sorry?" I asked as I cuddled him closer to me to soak up his warmth.

It was fall in South Dakota, and snow could start any minute. The temperatures were getting colder every night, and some mornings there had been frost on the grass. It wouldn't be long before snowflakes fluttered in the air.

"You're so full of shit! Why is warming you up my job?"

I nuzzled into Zac's neck and took in his smell because it was my favorite thing. "You love me. You don't want me to be cold, do you?"

Zac exhaled and got closer, just like I wanted. "How was Dakota when you left?" he asked.

I breathed out and slid lower so I could kiss his soft lips. At first, his lips were hard, but then he wrapped his arms around me, and we really kissed the way I liked it. Our tongues swirled together, and I heard him hum quietly—that was a good sign.

I tried to be gentle as I pulled him on top of me, happy we were both without clothes. It was my turn to hum. "Tell me why you left?" I whispered as I skimmed my nose over his neck. He was soft and smelled good. It was my favorite thing in the world.

Zac pulled back a little and rested his elbows on the mattress next to my ears as his hands held up his head. "I got scared. I know that sounds ridiculous because he's just a little boy, but I got the feeling your mom wants something more than for the three of us to be friends, and I don't think he liked me at all."

It was what I thought. "I think Mom's worried about what's gonna happen to Dakota because his grandpa is gonna die. He has cancer, and Martin has been taking him to doctors' appointments. Melvin is the boy's only living relative."

Zac sat up, letting cold air under the covers, which wasn't exactly to my liking. I liked how cozy it had been before he sat up.

"He doesn't have *any* family at all?" Zac asked, his voice sounding sad.

I pulled him down and settled him on my chest again. It was the best way to sleep, and I was tired. "His mother is dead. His grandpa is gonna die, and he doesn't have anybody else. I'd like us to be his friends, but if you don't think you can, then I'll tell Mom."

Zac pulled on my chest hair and sat up again. I didn't like the pulling at all. "No! Don't tell her that. Maybe just help me learn how to be around him?"

"If you stop hurting me, I'll help you," I told him as I pulled him back down to get some sleep. I knew Zac would make a wonderful dad for Dakota because he barely knew him and was already worried about the boy. It would just take the two of them some time to get used to each other.

Chapter Six

Zac

Sunday morning was cold and sunny, just as I expected in South Dakota in early October. It was still one of the most beautiful places I'd ever seen, though Niagara Falls was pretty damn lovely. Winter wasn't far away, but there were still some gorgeous, unexpectedly warm days left to enjoy. The weekend was turning out to be one of them.

I was sitting at the kitchen table doing research on my laptop when Gus rushed inside from the shop. He'd made a few more wooden toys for Dakota, and I could see he was excited to get to his mother's house.

My husband proudly held out the unpainted wooden toys—one of them was a little wagon, a tractor, and one that looked like a little peddle car. They all had wheels that spun around, and they were adorable.

"What time did you get up? You were gone when I woke," I asked as I sipped my coffee.

"Uh, I couldn't sleep later than five, and I didn't want to bug you, so I got up and went out to the shop to make these. I think Dakota will like them. What do you think? Are they stupid?"

Of course, they weren't stupid. They were so damn intricately put together that I was in awe of them. I wasn't sure, though, if Dakota would like them, because I didn't know what the child might or might not like. I hoped to hell Gus' feelings didn't get hurt. He'd been working on them for hours.

"I think they're great. I'm not sure what Dakota might think of them, but you should give them to him. Maybe he likes to paint things? That's a good thing, right?"

As I stared at my beautiful husband, I was consumed with fear. Keeping Gus from getting hurt by anyone was my priority, and I damn sure wouldn't stand by and watch it happen.

There was no way I could lie to Gus and say I instantly liked Dakota, but I couldn't say I didn't like him, either. I had no idea what the boy needed, and his reaction to seeing me the previous night gave me the feeling I never would.

I did know, however, that if Gus or his gifts were rejected by the boy, it would gut my guy. I also had the feeling I'd frightened the little guy so much that he'd never warm up to me, which would also crush Gus.

Gus and Monica were sure Dakota and I would get along well, but I refused to romanticize the situation. There would be a lot of work required from anyone who tried to help any child like Dakota, and I wasn't completely certain I had it in me.

There were challenges associated with his autism, but he'd also been abused by his mother, though we didn't exactly know how badly. How could anyone make that up to a little boy?

Educating myself about all the requirements to help a child with Dakota's challenges seemed like the best option. My biggest insecurity was that I wouldn't be able to do anything for Dakota that was close to what Monica had done for Gus. I had the feeling that was what everyone expected from me, and how would they feel if I let them down?

In my eyes—and in her son's—Monica was a saint. I was under no illusions anyone would ever say anything as kind about me.

A huge, selfish worry that had settled into the back of my mind was that if Dakota never learned to like me, would I be able to stand by and watch Angus spend time with the boy without me? Was I a big enough person to keep my jealousy at bay at having to share Angus?

No one would ever understand Dakota like Gus, so I couldn't impede Gus' support of the boy, but I had to wonder where it left me. As I saw it, I would be out in the cold—no pun intended because I lived in South Dakota.

"I, uh, my stomach is kinda queasy. Why don't you go over to your mom's place, and I'll just rest? If I feel better, I'll come over later. I might do a little work, too," I suggested, though I just had one contract pending, and the deadline wasn't for two weeks.

Gus studied me for a moment, and I felt exposed. My husband had a look he gave me when he could tell I wasn't being truthful with him, but he wasn't going to call me on it.

I saw it flash over his face just before he retrieved his phone from his pocket and pressed a few buttons.

"Son?" It was Monica. *What's he doing?*

"Hi, Mom. Zac doesn't feel good, so I'm gonna stay home with him." *Nooo!* I felt like the biggest asshole in the world.

"*Gus, no!* Go spend time with Dakota. I'll be fine, I swear," I stated quickly, moving close enough for Monica to hear me over the line... *hopefully*.

I didn't want him to stay home with me. That wasn't the goal. I just didn't want to try to bond with Dakota again so soon.

"Is he throwing up? Running a fever? Tummy troubles?" Monica quizzed, making me feel more horrible by the minute for trying to lie.

Gus had put it on speaker, and I was red from head to toe at the sound of concern in her voice. I stepped closer to Gus. "Monica, I'm fine. I just have a touch of a headache, but I'll be fine. We'll be over in a little while."

I punched the button to end the call and looked at Gus. "You did that on purpose."

He thought he was so clever, holding up his hands as if he was surrendering. "I wanted to stay home and take care of you if you felt bad. Dakota's got Mom. He'll be fine for today."

"You gave that boy your word that you'd be back, and you can't break it, Gus. You know how much you hated it when people disappointed you as a kid," I stated, glaring at him as I walked across the room.

"Okay, okay, but I won't leave you here by yourself if you don't feel well. You're my husband," Gus stated.

I walked back over to him and took his hands, holding them to my chest. "I love you. I want to support you, and you want to spend time with Dakota, so we'll go over to your mom's. I'll take my laptop and work while you hang out."

The triumphant smile on my husband's face was annoying as hell. "I want to talk to you about the book idea when Dakota's around. I think he could help us with it. Will you spend time with us, too?" Gus pushed.

I wanted to say I wasn't ready. That I needed time to dig into what Dakota's needs might be before I spent time with him. Not scaring the shit out of the boy was a good start.

"He's afraid of me, Gus. I don't want to be in the way of the two of you spending time together," I responded, leaving off the part where I was probably more afraid of the boy than he really was of me.

My fear stemmed from handling a random situation in a way that wasn't in Dakota's best interests that would upset him to the point he'd shut down on us. The goal was to help him recover the ground he'd lost when Mr. Standing Bear first became ill and there had to be changes in Dakota's routine. I couldn't live with myself if I was the cause of the boy continuing to withdraw.

I knew the two of them probably had many things in common, things I might never understand. When it came to the world I was sure they shared, I'd always be an outsider. Could I live with that?

Sitting on the hallway floor just outside of Gus's childhood bedroom with my laptop, I smiled as I glanced up to check on Gus and Dakota. I was editing a research paper about gene therapy for a college student—thank god all I had to do was pay attention to the paper structure, not the science. They had a technical reader for that type of editing.

As it was, I was having a hell of a time staying awake as I read it. No offense to the writer, but it was dry as sawdust—which was actually a smell I loved since I'd spent time in the wood shop with my handsome husband.

"Mr. Pugh's cow, Clara, was as tall as that dresser, and she had a little brown baby calf that followed her everywhere. Mr. Pugh let me go into the barn to leave a bale of hay for Clara because it was winter, and it was too cold for the two of them to be outside. The little calf—I called it Brownie—it would come over to me and wipe its milky froth on my coveralls after it got done eating, but it would let me pet it if I stood very still," Gus explained.

Dakota was sitting on the other side of the bed with Gus, leaning against the wall while being told a story about a baby calf my husband knew as a boy after Monica adopted him.

Gus was holding a framed drawing he'd taken from the wall as he told the story. I had tears in my eyes watching him tell the boy about something that was precious from Gus' childhood.

A pang of jealousy coursed through me as I watched the man I loved. I'd read the stories Gus had written, but he'd never told them to me the way he was telling them to Dakota. I was being so foolish; I felt like *I* needed to go sit in the corner.

Monica's footsteps were on the stairs, so I went back to work. When she arrived on the landing, she held out a cup of hot chocolate. "How do you feel, Zachary?" Her cocked eyebrow gave me the impression she was onto my sad excuse.

My stupid lie about feeling ill earlier in the day had me feeling so guilty that my stomach churned at her comment. "I'm fine, Monica," I answered as I accepted the mug from her.

She smiled and gave me a wink before she walked into the bedroom and put the tray on the bed, scooting it closer to Gus. There were two mugs of cocoa on it, plus a bowl of mini-marshmallows and chocolate chips. I knew Gus would be in heaven, but I was curious whether Dakota could be tempted by sweets.

"Can Zac come in and have hot chocolate with us?" Gus asked the boy. I could see his face over the top of the mattress, and I saw his eyes were crinkled as he gave Dakota a comforting smile.

There was a soft, whishing sound from under the bed. Gus slid up to his knees from his seat, glancing at me and winking. "You can't drink hot chocolate while you're lying on your belly. Come out and meet Zac."

Gus' face blossomed into a tender grin as he watched me. "Scoot inside on your cute butt and sit there by the closet, please."

I almost laughed at his compliment, but that might have been too much for the boy, so I didn't. I closed my laptop and put it on the floor, carefully sliding into the room with my hot chocolate in my right hand.

I settled against the closet door, and when Gus thought I was okay, he sat down on the floor where he could see both of us, his smile so beautiful it made my heart clench.

"Zac's in here, now. Come out. He wants to say hi," Gus coaxed. I secretly hoped the boy came out so Gus' smile didn't fade.

I saw no movement, so I stayed quiet, just watching Gus. He sat still and sipped his drink slowly, looking at me with my favorite smirk. I held up my mug in cheers and smiled in return, wondering how long the standoff was going to last.

Finally, Gus spoke... to me. His tone was gentle, and his voice was soft as silk, which made me mushy inside. "These pictures on the walls are from my stories. The one with the house is about when we moved in here with Martin and the neighbor's cat that used to come over through a hole in the fence. I kept fixing it, but the cat figured out how to get in, anyway. I was afraid he was going to get hit by a car, but he was very sneaky."

He pointed to another one as I grinned at him. "That's the story of the chickens Mom had for a while before she got tired of the mess they made in the yard. One was named Birdie. She used to eat out of my hand," Gus told me as he pointed to a colorful drawing with a white hen in the yard by a tree with a few little fuzzy yellow chicks around her.

"What happened to the chicks?" I whispered, trying not to disturb the quiet.

Gus chuckled. "Mom said she gave them good homes, but I figured out it was in our freezer when I got older. Oh, uh. Hello. Will you come sit over here so you can say hi to Zac? He's my husband, and he wants to meet you. I promise, he's a very nice man," Gus said as he looked down to his left and pointed to his right, which was directly across from me.

I put down my mug and situated myself in the least threatening way I could think of, and I waited. The top of a head filled with dark-brown hair peeked out around the bedspread with the cowboys on it, and that was when I saw there were no earmuffs as Gus had described.

As I was about to say hi, Gus shook his head, so I waited. "Let's come all the way out from under the bed and sit down over here so you can drink your hot chocolate. Monica made it especially for us." He wasn't talking to me, but then Dakota crawled over his lap and sat next to him with his back to me.

Gus' smile lit up the room. I was guessing it was progress, though it wasn't what I expected. My husband looked at me and nodded, so I cleared my throat and said hello.

"Hi, Dakota. I'm Zac. It's very nice to meet you."

That was all I said, and as I glanced at Gus—because the boy hadn't looked at me at all—my guy nodded and gave me a happy grin that touched me deep inside. His eyes sparkled, and Gus looked as happy as he had the day we got married on the boat under Niagara Falls. It was beautiful.

Maybe with Gus' help, could I figure it out? As I sat there staring at my sexy woodsman, I knew I wanted to try more than anything.

Chapter Seven

Zac

"They're here," Gus yelled from the backyard, causing my nerves to skyrocket.

God, I'd never survive if I had to go to court to be judged by a group of my peers. It couldn't be any worse than meeting Dakota's grandfather, could it?

I was in the kitchen cutting out peanut-butter-and-jelly sandwiches with animal-shaped cookie cutters that Monica had sent to the farm from an online kitchen company. I was guessing she believed I'd need them as part of her diabolical plan… whatever it was.

Gus had been busy building a small shed next to the workshop, though he wouldn't confess what it was supposed to be for. He said it was a surprise for me—and a surprise from Gus left me seven kinds of excited… and eight kinds of worried.

It was the weekend after our first meeting with Dakota, and I was petrified. Mr. Standing Bear was bringing the boy over so Gus could show him the things he did in the wood shop. After that, Gus was planning for the two of them to create some new illustrations for Gus' stories that he was thinking about allowing me to turn into children's books.

I was trying to decide if it would be best for us to self-publish them or go through a traditional publishing house. There were pros and cons to both routes, but before I proposed any ideas to Gus, I had to see how things progressed with Dakota.

Stepping out the back door to the concrete pad where Gus parked that rickety old truck, I saw Monica's small SUV. Mr. Standing Bear was next to the back passenger door, leaning against his cane as he waited for Dakota to get out.

Gus strolled over to the vehicle as calm as you please, climbing into the back seat with the boy. Monica, who was carrying a cake server and a cloth bag, led Mr. Standing Bear toward our house.

Seeing the woman with food made me smile because I was sure Monica wondered how her son and I could keep ourselves alive. I'd remind her how she'd taught Gus to cook, and how great he was at it. We were doing just fine.

"Please, come inside," I invited the two of them.

At some point in time, Mr. Standing Bear had been a tall man. I could see that he still had a lot of pride, so I didn't comment about the fact he was hunched over and used a cane, his frame quite thin. The man's face was weathered, but his eyes were kind as he grinned at me.

"Hello, sir. It's a pleasure to have you come by," I greeted as I took Monica's bundles. She helped Mr. Standing Bear up the three steps and onto our back porch, where he wiped his feet before he came inside.

The house was warm. Gus had insisted on building a fire in the living room fireplace, and for once, I hadn't argued about the mess he made. Gus had taught me how cozy a fire could make our home feel and how romantic it was to make love in front of one.

There was one problem—my husband always made a colossal mess when he stacked the logs and when he cleaned out the ashes. I walked around the house barefoot most of the time, and it hurt like hell to step on pieces of bark or wood chips.

Cozy was nice, but sometimes, Gus got carried away, and the fire was like being in a pizza oven—like at that very moment. I reached up and cracked a window in the corner of the kitchen over the sink where I'd been busy working with the sandwiches.

I took their coats and showed them into the living room, where Mr. Standing Bear took a seat at the end of the couch nearest the fire. "This feels nice," he said to no one in particular. *Maybe that was why Gus built the fire?*

Monica smiled and peeled off the turtleneck sweater she was wearing to reveal a long-sleeved t-shirt. She draped the sweater over the back of the couch and sat down at the other end. "At my age, you know, I have hot flashes. It's just a little too warm for me." I nodded in agreement—happy I'd put on a pair of loose track pants and a short-sleeved t-shirt.

My mother-in-law then turned to Mr. Standing Bear. "Melvin, this is my son-in-law, Zachary. Zac, this is Melvin Standing Bear. Why don't you sit down and chat while I go make us some coffee? I brought pineapple upside down cake and some Jell-O that I know Gus and Dakota both like," she said before she left me there with a dying man who just kept staring at me as if he thought I were going to steal the silver. I worried I had something hanging out of my nose, but it would be rude to get up to go check, wouldn't it?

"I, um..." *What the hell do you say to someone who looks like he could drop dead at any minute?*

"Where are you from?" the man asked.

"I, uh, I was born in Chicago. I believe my parents still live there. My mother's parents are from Kansas City. My, uh, grandma lived there when I was young, and I moved to New York to go to college." Thankfully, I got the words out without sounding like a stammering idiot through the whole thing.

"You got brothers or sisters?" Mr. Standing Bear asked.

"N-No. No more at home like me. I think I was a mistake because my parents didn't try again after they got me." It was the lamest joke I'd ever made, but I blurted it out without being able to stop it. Mr. Standing Bear just looked at me like there was something wrong with me. At that point, I wasn't sure he was wrong.

"Monica said you like to wear makeup. Why?" the man asked, taking me completely off guard.

I wasn't a praying man, but I truly prayed that Monica came back into the living room soon. Melvin was glaring at me, or so it seemed, and I was having a hard time putting together a sentence.

After a moment, I decided honesty was definitely the best policy. What did it hurt to answer the man's questions?

"I do sometimes. It makes me feel more confident when I'm feeling self-conscious. My husband is a very attractive man, and I don't want people to wonder what he's doing with me, so I want to look my very best when we go out," I answered, trying to joke again.

Mr. Standing Bear took me in, head to toe. "You look fine to me. How old are you?"

"I'm twenty-three, almost twenty-four," I answered.

"What do you do to make money?"

I exhaled. I was pretty sure my *curriculum vitae* wouldn't impress the man at all. "I'm a journalism major, but I edit and proofread books. I'd love to write a book of my own someday, but I haven't had that one great idea everyone talks about. For now, I help other writers publish their great ideas," I answered, pretty proud of myself for coming up with that on the fly. It wasn't a lie, either.

"Do you tell stories?" Mr. Standing Bear asked.

"Oh, no, sir. Gus is the storyteller in our family. He's definitely the artist between us. I just make sure he knows I love..." I was suddenly worried that the man might not be in favor of having his grandson hang around with two gay men, if that was the goal.

I had an inkling that Monica wanted help to watch Dakota or maybe when she became his guardian while Mr. Standing Bear was undergoing cancer treatment. I hoped to hell Monica had already discussed us with the man if we were going to be spending time with the little boy.

"Do you think you could love Dakota?"

I was taken aback for a moment. How in the world could I answer that question?

Thankfully, Monica came into the living room with a smile and a small plate of some sort of cookies. I glanced at her, my eyes getting big because of how much I was freaking out.

"Zac, these are piñon cookies. They're a shortbread type cookie made with pine nuts. Try one, won't you?" she suggested as she held the plate for me. I quickly took two and shoved one in my mouth to keep from having to answer.

Monica then turned to Mr. Standing Bear. "Melvin, Zac can't possibly declare that he loves Dakota yet. He doesn't even really know your grandson. But, he and Angus have a great capacity for love. You remember from Martin how difficult things were in the beginning between Gus and him. These things take time, and you know that. How long did it take you to spend time with Dakota and understand him?"

Mr. Standing Bear chuckled before he reached for a cookie. "You're too smart for me, Monica."

She laughed. "No, Melvin, I just understand what you're looking for... what assurance you need... but you're going to have to trust us. Dakota has a long road to travel, but I promise you, he will be loved. He's going to have a wonderful, loving family."

Thankfully, before I had to ask questions myself about what Monica meant by her comments, the back door opened and Gus came inside. "We take off our shoes here so we don't mess up the floors that Zac just cleaned this morning. We hang our coats here so they're not in the way. It smells good inside, doesn't it?"

"Mm-hmm."

Monica reached out and grabbed my hand, nearly making me spill my coffee. She looked at Melvin, who was still, too. In a heartbeat, there were tears on his cheeks, so he took off his glasses and sat there, gazing at the fire.

I glanced at Monica, who was also crying. It felt like a big moment, so I didn't say anything, not sure what I was missing.

"You want juice, or do you want milk?" Gus asked the boy. I heard cabinets opening and closing and a mug and a glass on the counter. I wanted to go help, but I didn't want to scare Dakota, so I stayed where I was.

"Milk." It was a quiet voice, but I could see how much it affected Mr. Standing Bear.

I turned to Monica for clarity. "It's the first time Dakota's answered a question where we could hear him. He talks to himself when he doesn't think anyone's around."

Oh...

Chapter Eight

Gus

I poured Dakota a glass of milk, seeing a small plate of cookies on the counter. "You wanna sit at the table?" I asked him. He pointed to a chair, so I carried our things over and pulled it out.

Dakota climbed into the chair and took his earmuffs from around his neck. I'd bought him a pair of noise-canceling headphones to use in the shop that he'd liked wearing, moving his earmuffs down to his neck. He'd smiled when he'd worn them because they matched the ones I used when working with power tools.

I'd shown him how some of the tools worked, and he'd watched with big eyes. I was glad I'd thought of the headphones because I knew the loud noises would be too much for him. There were days when they were too much for me, too.

"We can paint cars or we can draw pictures. I think—hang on a second," I said as I hopped up from my seat and went to the living room where Mom and Melvin were sitting. Zac was there, but he wasn't moving.

"Do I need to put on more wood?" I asked them as I pointed to the fireplace that wasn't blazing as much as it had been earlier when I'd stoked it. I'd swept up the mess I'd made because I didn't want Zac to be upset with me. He was trying to make a good impression on Mr. Standing Bear, so I cleaned up after myself for once.

Zac stood from his seat and wrapped his arms around my waist. He was sobbing before I knew it, and I was worried. I leaned forward and whispered, "What happened?"

Mom stood and hugged the two of us. “Nothing is wrong, Gus. We’re just happy.”

I glanced at Melvin to see he was crying too. *What the hell happened? I’ve only been outside for a little while.*

I put Zac back in his chair and sat down next to Melvin. “Do you feel sick? Would you like to rest? We have a spare room you can use. I can carry you if you don’t feel like walking,” I offered.

Poor Melvin looked kind of gray, and he didn’t weigh much. I felt awful for him, but that wouldn’t make anything better, would it?

Dakota’s grandfather smiled at me, though it was kinda sad. “I’m fine, Angus. Thank you for spending time with Dakota. I’ve never heard his voice that loud before.”

I turned to Mom to see her smile, too. When I glanced at Zac, he had tears on his face. “Is that good?” I wasn’t sure what to think.

Zac stood and kissed my cheek. “Yes, sweetheart. It’s very good.”

I knew he’d explain it to me later, so I took Zac’s hand and pulled him with me to the kitchen, pulling out the chair on the other side of mine so he was across from Dakota.

“Cookie?” I asked as I held the plate for Dakota, who took one, and then Zac, who took one, too.

The three of us sat quietly, eating the cookies and drinking our drinks. I was glad that Dakota hadn't gone under the table as I'd worried he might do. Seeing the two of them together in the same space made me very happy.

When Zac and I were in bed later that night, I asked, "Did you have fun today?" as he rested his head on my chest.

Dakota and I had worked on drawing pictures for the books Zac was going to make using my stories. It was a fun idea for the three of us to work on something together, and when Zac had agreed to help us, I was glad.

"I did. Was I okay with him? I mean, he didn't go under any furniture," Zac answered.

I laughed as I pulled him closer. "That was a good thing. I used to go under furniture a lot. I felt safer in close spaces. Is that weird?" I asked.

Zac kissed my chest. "Not at all. It explains a lot, though."

I glanced down to see his smile, and it made me feel good. "What does it explain?"

"It's why you love to sleep close. You feel good with the two of us wrapped around each other, and I love it, too. I feel loved when you hold me," Zac whispered.

I liked that answer. "Thank you. I feel the same. You know I love you and we're going to have a good life, right?"

Being in the workshop with Dakota as we sanded the little cars was nice. I talked and he nodded, which was a step forward with him. I remembered being his age and not wanting to talk to anyone because I lived in a group home. It was like nobody listened, anyway.

Zac sat up, taking the warm covers away from me again, but I didn't complain. He was serious about something, and I wanted to know what he had to say.

"I don't know if I'll be the best person to help him, Gus. I'm really selfish, you know. I don't think he likes me, and I don't know how to change his mind." I could see Zac was worried, so I pulled him down and covered us again.

"You found a way to love me, Zac. It might take time with Dakota, but that's okay. Mom's happy to give him a home until we're ready," I answered.

Zac sat up, taking the covers--*again*. "Ready for what?"

I glanced at the clock to see it was nearly midnight, and I had an order for cabinets at a store in town. I needed to sleep—unless Zac wanted to make love. I reached down to touch his dick, finding it soft, so I guessed that wasn't going to happen.

"I need to get some sleep. I have cabinets to make for Hardy's, remember?" I reminded him.

Zac exhaled. "Okay. Good night."

He turned his back to me and snuggled into my body, just as I wanted. "Night."

Chapter Nine

Zac

"Happy Halloween," Gus told me, dangling a wood-carved skeleton in front of me as I finished my latest job editing a blog article. I hit the send button and glanced up at my husband.

"That's adorable," I told him as I studied the intricately carved parts that were interlocking without visible breaks. It was so fucking cool, and the kiss on my neck made it that much better.

"I made this one for you and a little bat for Dakota with wings that move when you bounce it. It's kinda like a puppet. I thought we could go get Dakota at Melvin's and take him to Mom's house to carve some jack-o'-lanterns for her front porch. We can take a walk later this afternoon before it gets dark so he can see the decorations in her neighborhood ahead of all the kids trick-or-treating. He won't want to be out with the crowd, but he can sit inside with Mom while we give out candy. He might enjoy seeing the costumes," Gus suggested.

Turning in my chair, I saw how excited Gus seemed to be, which was a surprise. "Did you ever go trick-or-treating?"

Gus kneeled on the kitchen floor in front of my chair and kissed me, his soft lips making me want more. I knew, however, he had plans for the rest of the day, so I could wait.

"Mom used to sit outside on the porch with me so I could watch, but I couldn't imagine going to a stranger's door and knocking to ask for candy," he responded, his answer making my heart clinch in my chest.

I reached out to touch his handsome cheek. His beard was growing back, as was his gorgeous hair, and my heart-beat quickened at how much I loved him. I didn't think one lifetime with Angus McMurray would be enough.

"Did you go out? I bet you looked cute in a costume," Gus teased as he tickled my ribs, making me squirm and giggle.

"I went out with kids from school when I was younger. When I was older, I saw it as an opportunity to sparkle," I joked as I offered jazz hands. Gus chuckled at me.

"I think you're beautiful no matter what, but if you want us to dress up as something before we go to Mom's, I'll let you make me up, too. I've never dressed up for Hal-loween before." Gus had a dazzling smile, and my mind raced with a million ideas.

"If you want to dress up, we can. That might be fun! Nothing too scary, though, right?" I asked.

Gus's eyes lit up. "You will?"

"Oh, sweetheart, we can definitely dress up! Let's go upstairs and figure out what we want to be," I invited.

Gus stood and whisked me up in his powerful arms, yet again, turning me to goo in his grasp. He carried me to our room, and before we figured out costumes, Gus reminded me how much we loved each other.

I struck gold when I searched through Gus' closet, finding a straw hat that Gus said he used when he worked on the roof. Dressing him up as a scarecrow, I drew a cute smile and some little freckles on his handsome face. There was even a ladybug on his cheek. He looked beyond amazing.

Then, Gus created my costume, and when he reached into my panty drawer and pulled out a pair of black lace panties with a ribbon crisscrossing my ass, I stared at him, and he started cracking up, using the dresser to hold himself up.

"I'm thrilled to amuse you. What do you think you're going to dress me up like? A whore?" I teased him. He was so joyful of late that I just couldn't get over it.

"No. These are just for me," Gus teased as he went into one of his drawers and pulled out a bright orange hoodie. He went into my drawer and grabbed a pair of my black skinny jeans.

"Put these on. I'll be back," he ordered before he hurried out of the house, across the yard, and into the shop. I pulled a thermal shirt on under the hoodie and grabbed a pair of socks and my black sneakers, heading to the kitchen to wait.

Five minutes later, Gus came inside with a roll of black tape. "What's that for?"

"Gonna make you a pumpkin... *pumpkin*," Gus joked.

He took the sweatshirt from me and whisked it over my body before he put me on the kitchen table. "Lay down," he insisted, so I did. There wasn't much I wouldn't do for the man.

"Should we stop at the store and get something for Dakota?" I asked as Gus tore strips of black tape and put them on the sweatshirt as he stood between my legs. His tongue was sticking out between his lips as he concentrated.

"You better be careful, scarecrow. You might bite that tongue off, and that would make me very unhappy," I teased him.

Gus didn't even flinch, continuing to tear off strips of tape and attach them to the shirt. "Maybe we should check with your mom to see if she wants us to stop by the store?"

Nothing.

"*Angus!*" I whined, studying his face to see he was trying to hold back a smirk, the smartass.

He laughed and put the tape on the table, holding out his hand to help me sit up before he put me on the floor. I turned in a slow circle for him to look at me, and when he grinned, I waited for him to comment. "Your face needs to be green like the handle on the top of the pumpkin."

I laughed. "I don't have anything green to put on my face, Gus," I responded. We hadn't thought about dressing up, so we were improvising.

Gus smirked and left the kitchen while I put on my socks and shoes before going to the back door to see it was flurrying just a little. Hopefully, it wouldn't amount to anything.

I heard Gus return to the kitchen with a green stocking cap and a jar, along with a white pillowcase. "I hate a hat," I complained.

From behind his back, Gus showed me the jar of my pore refining green mask that he'd caught me wearing as I soaked in the tub one night while he was watching a hockey game. He'd laughed and laughed at me.

"No."

"Please?"

"No. That's a private thing that I do so I look good when we go out. Nobody likes to see pores the size of craters," I protested.

"I'm wearing makeup. With the hat and the gross stuff, you'll look so cute. Who can be afraid of a smiling jack-o'-lantern?" Gus asked, giving me his puppy-dog eyes.

God, I would never win a battle in my life, I was sure. "*Fine.*"

I took the cream from him and read the back to ensure it wouldn't take off my face if I left it on for more than an hour, and then I went into our bathroom and slathered a thin layer of the stuff on my face.

I grabbed my moisturizing serum to take with me for when I washed it off and then I pulled on the ugly Kelly-green stocking cap and went out to the kitchen to see Gus holding up the white pillowcase.

He'd made two round eyes and a crooked smile out of the electrical tape. "What about the arms?" I asked him, seeing his proud grin.

"I'll wait to cut them until we get there and I can measure him," Gus informed, which was the logical answer.

We got into the rickety truck and Gus stopped at the little bakery down the street from End of the Trail to pick up a few dozen iced cookies, along with an iced mocha coffee for me. I kissed his cheek, being careful not to get green on the great makeup job I'd done on his handsome face.

We drove to Monica and Martin's house, and I saw there were a few houses in the neighborhood that had really decorated for the occasion. "Wow," I said.

"Yeah, that's why I thought we could walk around with him now and then we can move the couch so he and Mom can watch out the window while we give out candy. Maybe next year or the year after that, he'll want to go out for a bit to get his own candy. I'd really love that," Gus stated, his voice quiet. Turning to see him staring out the front of the truck, I smiled at the wistful grin on his face.

My heartfelt hope was that Mr. Standing Bear lived that long, as well. Dakota would be nine by next Halloween, and maybe with Gus as his friend, he'd come out of his shell enough that we could take him out for a short time. I believed if Gus wanted it to happen, it definitely would.

We both stepped out of the truck on either side. I saw four pumpkins on the back patio, along with a few chairs, a firepit, a large metal bowl, and a white bucket. Martin was sitting outside with Mr. Standing Bear as the two of them were laughing about something—probably me.

I grabbed the bag of cookies and followed Gus as he walked up to the patio. "Hello, Martin. Hey Mr. Standing Bear. How are you, sir?"

I stepped up behind Gus and saw Martin chuckle. "Hey, pumpkin."

"Ha-ha," I responded as I walked over to him. He stood and hugged me from a distance, not wanting to get the crap on my face all over his shirt.

"You look cute, and I see you got this guy to dress up. That's a first," Martin said as Gus actually hugged him. I could see the surprise on Martin's face, and I wondered why. I'd have to wait until Gus was occupied to ask Martin about it.

"Monica and Dakota are inside, and I think they've both been waiting for you," Martin told us, so Gus and I went inside.

My sweet husband opened the door for me, and when I went into the kitchen, I saw Monica's bright smile. "Aw! My boys look so cute." I rolled my eyes, because, come on! I looked stupid.

Gus walked over to her and gave her a hug. "How's my makeup? Pumpkin did it." Monica laughed as she hugged him in return.

"You look like the real deal, Angus."

She then turned to me and gave me a hug, trying not to muss her pretty rust-colored sweater with my green gunk. "Dakota is in the living room. Can I go get him?" she asked.

Gus grinned. "I made this for him. Do you think he'll wear it? Zac and I thought we could walk him around so he can see the different decorations in the neighborhood before dark, then you can sit with him in the living room so he can watch while we give out candy."

Monica jumped a little and clapped her hands, which was really a bit unsettling to see from a grown woman. "Oh, how cute! That's a great idea, Angus."

"We brought some cookies," I said as I put the bag on the counter.

Gus stepped closer to her and sniffed, which made me laugh. He was always checking whether Monica was still smoking, but I had the feeling she'd lived up to her end of the deal and had quit. Gus' smile confirmed it.

He kissed Monica's cheek and stepped back. "I'm proud of you, Mom. I don't want you to end up like Mr. Standing Bear." He pointed toward the patio where the man was smoking, and I understood his comment.

"Go get Dakota. He's in your room," Monica said.

Gus hurried off and left me with his mother. "How's Mr. Standing Bear doing?"

Monica went to the counter and grabbed a glass before she turned to me. "Would you like some lemonade, or maybe something else? My son looks so cute. I won't ask how you talked him into it," she joked.

I giggled. "It was actually his idea. He talked *me* into it, if you must know."

Monica opened the freezer and retrieved a storage container with red cubes that she put in my glass before putting some in her glass, too.

After Monica poured in the sparkling lemonade she knew I loved, she stirred both of our drinks with swirly straws and handed a glass to me. “I think we need to have a talk, Zachary.”

That got my attention.

Chapter Ten

Gus

I followed Dakota downstairs after he let me help him into his ghost costume. I'd cut the hole at the bottom of the pillowcase for his head to go through and the armholes after I made sure he had on a sweatshirt beneath it so he'd be warm. He looked really cute.

"Do you like my costume?" I asked my new friend as he carried the little pickup truck we'd painted together. Dakota nodded and gave me a smile.

I then asked him, "How about your costume? Do you like it?"

Dakota nodded, stopping at the bottom of the stairs as I stepped next to him. "Do you wanna see Zac's costume?" I asked him.

His eyes traveled up my large body, and he pulled away, looking a little unhappy. "Do you want me to pick you up?" I asked.

I watched Dakota as he thought about it, so I kneeled down in front of him. "We want to have fun tonight, and we want you to come with us. We were going to walk down the street so we could see the decorations, and then we'll come back and you can watch the kids out the window," I explained to him.

Dakota turned his head to look out the window in the living room for a few seconds. He then held his arms up to me, so I picked him up. "Ready to see Zac?" I asked. He smiled at me, so we went into the kitchen where Mom and Zac were drinking something that looked pretty good.

"What's that?" I asked as I put Dakota into a chair before I sat down next to him.

"Frozen strawberry lemonade. Would you like some?" Zac asked. I glanced to see Dakota was staring at Zac's green face, which looked so cute.

"I'll have some. Kota?" I asked my little friend.

Dakota turned to look at me and grinned. "Yes."

Mom squeaked a little, and Zac got busy making Dakota a small frozen lemonade, complete with a crazy straw like he and mom were using.

The boy stared at me for a minute before he looked back at Zac, then at me, again. "Oh—that's Zac. He's a jack-o'-lantern. Do you want to carve some pumpkins for the front porch?" I asked him.

My Zac smiled and gave Dakota a little wave. I was thrilled when he waved in return. That was a big step for someone like us.

We walked the neighborhood first. Zac was on my left holding my hand, and Dakota was on my right wearing his pillowcase ghost costume and his earmuffs, his eyes moving quickly to take in everything.

We stopped at the first decorated house and I kneeled down next to Dakota. "This is where Mr. and Mrs. Girard live. Those are ghosts like you." He turned from the tree where the ghosts were hanging to stare at me, his little face squinched up in confusion.

"I don't think he heard all of it through the earmuffs," Zac suggested as he pulled out his phone and took a few pictures of the decorations, probably to send to his friend, Luke, who was still in graduate school in Philadelphia. They talked on video calls sometimes, but Luke was too busy to come visit Zac. I knew it made him sad.

I touched the earmuffs, and Dakota slid them onto his neck, so I repeated myself. He took my hand and led me closer to the front picket fence, so I picked him up to get a better look, showing him all the little ghosts hanging from the leafless tree branches.

Zac continued snapping pictures of the neighborhood, and in one of them, he got close to us and held up the phone for a selfie. He then showed it to me and Dakota, and I was surprised as I stared at the picture. I could see the three of us together as a family, just like I wanted since I'd met Zac. It was the best thing in the world.

"Can you send that picture to me?" I asked my husband, who winked and nodded.

We moved on toward the next house down the street and then one on the other side, but the farther down we went, the scarier the decorations were, so I turned to Dakota who was walking between us now, holding both of our hands.

I decided it was getting late enough that maybe we should head back to Mom's before the kids started coming out. "Think we should go back and have some cookies? We can show Monica the pictures Zac took." My two guys nodded, so we turned to go home.

I glanced around the neighborhood, not realizing how far down the street we'd gone and where we were on the street. I saw the next house, and I knew there was going to be a problem. As we approached, the Stiverson's rottweiler, Buster, came flying around the house and up to the fence, barking his fool head off like always.

Dakota started screaming and stiffened, putting his hands over his ears while the dog continued to go nuts, barking and running along the fence. I'd never liked that stupid dog. "*Stop it!*" Zac yelled at the mutt, but the thing kept going.

I, too, was frozen there in the street, but not from fear like Dakota, who continued to scream and had now started crying. Zac hurried to put his earmuffs over his ears, and then he picked up the boy and ran toward my mother's house.

I followed behind them, finally catching up to them to take Dakota from him so we could run faster. I wasn't thinking when we got that far down the street about that damn dog. That was my bad.

At least Zac knew what to do, because at that moment, I didn't. When we got to Mom and Martin's house, I ran straight inside with Dakota and handed the boy to my mom before I ran back outside to check on Zac, who was standing on the sidewalk, his green face with streaks through the green goo where he'd been crying, too.

I pulled him into my arms and held him close. "I'm so sorry. I didn't know what to do," I whispered to him as I rocked him in my arms. I hadn't exhibited very good parenting behavior. I'd definitely need to ask Mom how I could keep from messing up like that again.

Zac and I stood outside for quite a while, just holding each other. He turned his face up to mine. "I felt so helpless to keep him from being upset. I don't think I've ever had that reaction before, you know? Is he okay?"

"Yeah. I gave him to Mom so I could come check on you. Things like that—stupid mean dogs—happen every day. When something unexpected happens, people like me and Dakota, we have meltdowns. I used to have them all the time at the group home, and in that sort of place, one kid screaming usually leads to a bunch of kids screaming.

It seemed endless, sometimes," I explained to him. He needed to know what to expect if we were ever going to... if my dream was ever going to come true.

"Boys, are you okay?"

The back door opened, and I glanced up to see Mom coming outside. She was pulling her coat around herself as she met the cold air and snowflakes that were falling.

"Where's Dakota?" I asked her as I walked over to where she stood.

Taking her in, I remembered how lucky I'd always felt to have my mom. She was kind, caring, strict when she needed to be, but the thing I remember the most about Monica McMurray was how much she loved the people in her world. I was lucky to be one of them, and it took me a long time to see it, but now that I did, I appreciated it.

"He wanted to take a nap, so I put him in your bed and let him snuggle under the covers in his ghost costume. You guys wore him out, which probably magnified his meltdown. What triggered him?" Mom asked.

I sighed. "The Stiverson's stupid dog. I didn't realize we'd gone that far down the street. It came running up to the fence like usual and scared him," I told her.

Mom's mouth went into an angry, thin line. "I'm going to call animal control on that thing. They have no business having that kind of dog in the city limits. Come inside. It's too cold to stand out here."

She put her arm around Zac's shoulders—they were about the same height—and guided him toward the house. I followed behind and helped him take off his shoes by the front door where I left my boots, too.

When we stepped into the kitchen, Zac said, "I'm going to go wash my face. I'll be back." He went upstairs to use the bathroom across from my old bedroom, his footsteps quiet on the stairs.

"What did I do wrong? Could I have kept that from happening?" I asked Mom.

Mom shook her head. "Angus, you know yourself that sometimes things happened that scared you. You can't protect Dakota from every loud noise and barking dog in the world. Believe me, son, I tried to do it with you, and it's impossible."

I remembered how much Mom had tried to shield me from anything she believed might hurt me when I was younger. She was right. It was impractical to think someone could keep your kids from all the bad in the world, but with people like Dakota and me, I understood why parents were so set on trying.

"I want us to take him to therapy. I think it would help Zac understand better if he saw it for himself," I said.

Mom smiled and walked around the counter to hug me, which was the best. Good for me that now I had two people in my life who did.

Zac and I had been taking Dakota to his occupational therapy classes three times a week for the last month. It was just after Thanksgiving, which we didn't celebrate out of respect for Martin, and Zac had asked that I let him off at the shopping mall near the building where Elite Pediatric Services was located so he could get some Christmas presents. Of course, I didn't argue.

Once he was gone, I glanced across the bench seat where Dakota sat in a safety seat—he was small for his age, but it was because his mother took drugs—staring at the toy truck he'd painted just like my truck. "You ready to go to school?" I asked him.

That was what Mom and Melvin called his sessions with his therapist at Elite, and I remembered that was what Mom had called it when I used to go... "extra better school." I didn't find it better, really, but it was a school for me when I was young until I went to Scotland High—which wasn't better at all. Thankfully, I graduated, and Mom and Martin clapped louder than everyone else when I walked across the stage that day.

Dakota turned his eyes to the empty spot next to me where Zac usually sat. "Where he?" he asked as he pointed to Zac's spot.

Dakota hadn't been paying attention when we dropped Zac at the mall and hadn't noticed when he'd gotten out of the truck. I thought it was good that he wanted to know where Zac had gone. That was a step in the right direction.

"He went shopping. After school, you and I are gonna do some shopping of our own. Ready?" I said. Dakota nodded his head, and I drove us to the medical complex. While he was working with his therapist, I looked up car sales lots on my phone. It was time to get a better truck so we could all be comfortable and safe. And I was buying an automatic so Zac could drive it, too. No more burning clutches.

Chapter Eleven

Zac

We were at home on the farm, Gus working on the cabinet order for Hardy's Dry Goods in Scotland and me sitting at the kitchen table with Gus' notebooks as I typed up the stories he'd written since Monica had deleted them from her computer.

My husband's turn of phrase was sometimes awkward, but that was actually what made the stories that much more endearing and relatable for kids. I was planning to send the first story—Mike and Me—to Paula Pollard, my former boss' twin sister. Maybe it was a bitch move for me not to send it to Penelope Prentiss, but I still didn't like the woman even though she'd been the one to send me in Gus' direction.

I heard stomping on the porch steps, which was my Gus ridding his boots of the snow. It had snowed ten inches yesterday and overnight, and even though he'd shoveled a path and plowed the driveway, it came in on the bottom of his boots, and I'd already mopped the kitchen floor twice that morning.

"I hate taking them off if I just need to run inside for coffee," he'd complained.

"I hate getting out of the shower, only to have you get frisky and wanna make love again. When we finish, I've got your cum dripping down my legs such that I have to take another shower before I can start my day, but I still do it," I'd responded.

Of course, Gus had laughed, given me kisses all over my face, and now he was standing on the top of the back stairs unlacing his boots. That was a coup for me.

"Hey, sweetheart. Are you hungry?" I asked him as I saved a story onto a thumb drive to take to the shop office to print. If I hadn't bought the printer and put it in the shop for the cabinet and woodworking business, Gus would still go to his mother's house to use her computer. Old habits were very hard for Gus to break.

"I could eat. Do you feel like going sleigh riding this afternoon? I can make a little track for us, and I'll go to Mom's and get the sleds," Gus suggested.

I turned around in my chair and studied his face. He was about to bust with excitement, which meant there was something else. "And then maybe you go to Melvin's and pick up Dakota to bring him over?" I asked, seeing the excitement he'd been trying to hide come bubbling forth.

His smile split his face in a heartbeat, and he was nearly vibrating with happiness. Melvin had finished his chemo and was a little better, it seemed. We were still taking Dakota to occupational therapy, but his tutoring sessions took place at Melvin's house now that he was feeling better.

I glanced out the window in the kitchen to see the new, used pickup he'd bought without me the previous month—a 2010 dual-cab Chevy Silverado in bright red—idling in the driveway near the back door.

I'd have been pissed about him doing it alone, but I didn't know anything about vehicles, so we skipped the fight. It was clean and in mint condition, so I could find nothing to complain about. Once I thought about it and remembered how picky he really was, I was relieved I didn't have to shop with him.

I chuckled. "Give me a minute to change into jeans and a sweater, and I'll come with you. We can stop at the diner and get lunch on the way," I suggested.

When I heard Gus' heavy footsteps in the hallway behind me, I knew it would take more than a minute. "Gus, aren't you hungry?" I asked him, stopping outside the bedroom door.

He had already left his coveralls downstairs and was standing in his long underwear and his typical flannel shirt and wool socks. Oh, he looked yummy.

Gus picked me up, so I was glued to his front like a koala. I wrapped my arms and legs around him and hung on. "I like all your ideas, you know," he told me as he crawled onto our unmade bed. I hadn't gotten around to making it yet because I was eager to send the draft off to Paula, and now I was happy I hadn't.

He put a bit of his weight on me as he rested over me. He was solid, my husband, and I loved every inch of him.

"Are you going to help me make the bed when we're done?" I asked as Gus raised up on his knees and unbuttoned his red-and-black shirt. He looked like Mr. December in some lumberjack calendar, and I knew I was lucky to have him. All those other bitches out there would be green with envy if they had Gus take them to bed, I was certain.

"I'll help you change the sheets after," he told me, chuckling as he shucked off both the flannel and thermal shirts before he reached for my sweatshirt and pulled it over my head.

Not a lot of prep was needed because we'd already made love that morning—second shower and all. Gus easily slid inside me after he lubed both of us, and he stopped, staring into my eyes.

"You are more than I ever deserve, and I almost feel selfish asking for something else," he whispered into my ear as he slowly pumped into me. That piqued my interest.

"Honey, I love you. I'll give you the world, if I can," I answered, enjoying the feel of our skin rubbing together. The soft scratch of his chest hair felt good to me. Hell, everything about Gus felt good to me.

Gus picked up the pace and rolled us over such that I was on top of him. His cock inside me made it hard to keep from groaning like a whore, but Gus was usually quiet during sex, though he would whisper how good it felt to be inside me and how much he loved me.

I leaned forward and swiped my tongue over his mouth. He quickly captured my lips and wrapped his arms around me, holding me gently in his arms as we continued to move together. It felt like heaven to me, and my woodsman rang my bell perfectly.

His warmth spilled inside me, reminding me there was a third shower of the day in my future, but I really didn't care. He needed to show me how much he loved me, not just tell me, and I'd never grow tired of it.

"You wanna shower with me?" I asked him as I rested on his chest, the two of us sticking together from my jizz between us.

Gus pushed me up a little until my elbows were resting on his chest and we were gazing into each other's eyes like lovesick teens. We giggled at the same time.

"I want to ask you something, but I don't know how you'll feel about it, so I wanted to make love with you first because you might not want to make love with me again after," he said, his voice quiet and serious.

I smirked at him. "You know that's never going to happen, right? I love you. I'd never be so mad at you that I wouldn't want to make love. What's wrong?"

"Mom thinks it's time," he answered. I wasn't sure what Monica thought it was time to do, but I had a feeling it was going to be something that would change our lives forever.

"You talked to your mother about this instead of talking to me?" I asked, still not knowing what *this* was.

"No, Zac, I'd never do that. I called Mom while I was working on the cabinets this morning, and I asked how Melvin was doing. Mom said he's not doing well. He and Dakota are staying with her and Martin. Mom thinks Melvin's going to die soon," Gus told me.

I sat up and climbed off of him, sitting on the messy sheets we were going to be changing, anyway. The news actually broke my heart.

"Oh… God, that's horrible. What's going to happen to Dakota? Will Monica keep him?" I asked.

Gus sat up and took my left hand, kissing the band he'd carved for me that matched the one on his finger. He stared into my eyes and swallowed. "I was hoping we could adopt him. If Melvin is still alive, it'll be a lot easier."

I nearly swallowed my tongue, but then it occurred to me this was Gus' plan all along. He wanted to give me time to get comfortable around Dakota, even though I was sure the boy would never be comfortable with me.

Though… On Halloween, I hadn't hesitated for an instant before grabbing him up and taking off when that dog lost its fucking mind. When we took him for his OT, I was proud of him when the therapist told us he'd participated in whatever activity they'd set up for the day. When we had him over, he'd bring his papers from his tutoring sessions when he'd done a good job. Those papers now covered the front of our fridge, and every time I went to get something, I looked at them and my chest popped.

I reminded myself I wasn't his parent and considered that I might have to walk on eggshells around the boy to keep from upsetting him. Could I live that way for the rest of my life?

We didn't talk about it anymore. I hadn't even said a word to Gus since he'd mentioned the "A" word. It wasn't fair to ice him out, but I had a lot of thinking to do.

When we arrived at Monica's house, I saw Martin's work truck parked in the driveway behind the house, and I knew who I needed to talk to. We slipped off our boots and went inside, seeing Monica on the back porch with a find-a-word puzzle book.

"Is Martin here?" I asked her, not even greeting the woman as I usually did.

"He's in the living room watching the noon news. Are you boys hungry?" Monica asked, studying me without blinking.

I didn't answer. I went straight inside and through to the living room where Martin was sitting in his chair. Melvin was reclined on the couch, and he was quite pale. My heart skipped a beat. How could he be so calm? He was going to die any day now, and he was just watching the news?

"Where's Dakota?" I asked.

Just then, there were running feet on the stairs. "Ngus! Ngus!" we all heard.

I watched as he ran into the living room and scanned it for the one face he longed to see. "Ngus?"

"Back porch with Monica," I answered. He took off like a shot, and it was unbelievable to see him so excited.

"I bet he saw the truck he got to help Gus pick out," Melvin said. "He talks about picking the color. It's his favorite. He painted that little wooden truck red, and now you and Gus have a truck the same color."

I smiled at Melvin. "Yeah, Gus told me how happy he was at the dealership when the salesman brought it over for Gus to test drive it. I was Christmas shopping."

I hoped I didn't sound pissed off about the fact Gus had chosen it without me. I prayed to heaven I wasn't so damn selfish that I was jealous of a little boy with autism.

I absolutely refused to be so fucking shallow that I was jealous of a sweet little boy with a few challenges who had all of my husband's attention when he was around. I was a better human than that, wasn't I?

Gus took Dakota outside with him to find sleds while I got things ready for us to go over to the farm for sleigh riding. I was honestly scared to be left alone with Dakota, but I couldn't say it to my husband.

"Can I come in?" Martin asked. I was a bit relieved it was him and not Monica, so I nodded.

"I understand how you feel right now, Zac. I remember how afraid I was the first time Monica asked if she could leave me alone with Gus while she ran some errands. I'd spent time with her and Gus while we were dating, and I knew some of his triggers, so I said yeah, sure. We'd been married for a couple of weeks, and I figured I could handle anything the kid dished out," Martin explained.

I had to wonder if he knew something was up with me when I'd come into the living room to talk to him. I'd wanted to ask him how things were for him and Gus in the beginning, though I hadn't expected Melvin to be in there.

Gus wanted us to take Dakota and raise him. He'd been focused on the two of us starting a family, which was a noble idea, but I didn't know if I was ready for the responsibility. Where that left Gus and me, I really didn't know.

"How'd it go?" I asked Martin, who grinned.

"Just as bad as you'd imagine. Monica hadn't told him she was going, and when he saw me, he had a fit and barricaded himself in the basement, going so far as to nail the door shut from the inside. I begged and pleaded with him to let me in because I had my tools down there and I worried he'd get hurt. I sat on the floor in the kitchen and tried to talk him into taking out the nails so I didn't have to break down the door, and then a savior came along," Martin said.

Of course, by then, I was sucked in. "Who?" I asked as I put some dry clothes into a little tote bag for Dakota to put on after we went sledding.

"Not who—what. It was Mike. He was barking on the porch, and I let him in. Oh, there was hell to pay when Monica got home because she'd tried to chase that dog away so many times, but I put my foot down and the dog stayed. Four-hundred-dollars later, Gus had a dog who was flea and disease free. Gus and I had to clean up after him, but that dog did so much good for Gus. Hell, I hated it when Gus gave Mike to the Billings boy when they were moving to Nebraska," Martin explained.

Having just edited that story in particular, I was touched, but then I remembered the Stiverson's dog. "I don't think Dakota would enjoy being around a dog."

Martin smiled. "No, but maybe he and George can become friends? I still think it's good for Dakota to stay here with Mel as long as he can, but maybe you come over more and let the boy get used to you without Gus being around?"

I smiled at him. "That's easier said than done," I joked, which was the truth.

"Let me see if I can help with that, okay?" the man asked. I nodded, happy for any help he could give.

Chapter Twelve

Gus

I'd used the tractor to blade a level slope down the hill behind the barn. It was just steep enough to get a little speed, and Martin had even let me borrow two pairs of his snowshoes and the disk I used to use if we wanted to go snow trekking. It was a good way to introduce the idea of sledding to Dakota, and I was looking forward to it.

"Will you ride down with me?" I asked Zac.

He'd been silent after we'd left Mom and Martin's, eating leftover eggplant lasagna with them for lunch instead of stopping at the diner, and I wasn't sure what to say to him. Was he upset because we had stayed to eat at Mom's? He hadn't acted upset when we all sat down at the table, but I wasn't sure what to make of things.

"I thought maybe Dakota could ride on the disc and I could pull him up the hill where you and he could ride down. I need to get some exercise before I get fat from your mother's delicious lasagna."

I laughed at him and reached for his hand, holding it in mine on the console of the new truck. That was the only thing I didn't like about it. Gus couldn't sit next to me any longer because of the bucket seats, but as I glanced in the rearview mirror, I could see Dakota was safe in his booster in the back seat, which was what I'd wanted when I bought the truck.

"When do you want to get a Christmas tree?" Zac asked. It was ten days before Christmas, and it would be our second Christmas together. I hadn't bought a gift for Zac yet, but I needed to figure out what to get him. I knew I'd get him some of those sexy panties we both liked him to wear, but I wasn't good at picking out clothes for him. I had to give it some thought.

"We can get one from the tree lot outside town unless you want to go into the woods and try to find one," I offered. There were several pine trees back there that wouldn't be great for inside the house, but maybe we could put one in the yard?

"Let's think about it, okay?"

I walked around the truck and opened Zac's door, offering my hand to help him out. Before I could step away to open the door and let Dakota out of his seat, Zac held my hand. He kissed it, which surprised me.

"This is the life you want, right? You want Dakota to be a part of our family, don't you? Why didn't you tell me?" Zac asked.

I glanced at Dakota in the back seat as he played with the wheels of the little truck. I should have told Zac outright, but I wasn't sure how. That was something my mom never taught me.

"I hoped that you and Dakota would get to know each other and you'd see how much I love each of you. I'm sorry if I did this wrong," I responded.

Zac smiled at me. "You didn't do anything wrong. Let's get him out and have a great snow party."

It was the best news I'd heard in a while.

The smile on Dakota's face made my heart warm. Zac volunteered to pull Dakota up the hill on the disk, and they both looked like they were having fun. I rode down the small hill on the sled with Dakota, and when we got about halfway, there stood my Zac with his phone pointed toward us. He was laughing and waving at us, so we waved back as he took our picture.

When we got to the bottom, I turned to Dakota. "You wanna have Zac take you back up the hill? I'll meet you at the top."

Dakota glanced at me and then at Zac. For a second, he headed toward me, but then he smiled brightly, pulled up his earmuffs and slowly walked over to Zac.

"Up?" Dakota asked, and after a second, Zac laughed and helped him onto the disk, grabbing the rope and pulling it behind him to the top of the hill.

I picked up the sled and carried it with me, watching as Zac talked to Dakota while they headed to the top. Seeing them laughing together was a gigantic relief.

We played in the snow until it was almost dark. Zac had made a fire in the firepit, and we roasted vegetarian hotdogs over the flames.

"Ketchup or mustard on yours?" Zac asked, holding up the bottles for Dakota to choose.

"This," Dakota said, pointing to the mustard. I stopped Zac as he was about to squeeze it into the bun.

"What is that?" I asked Dakota. His ability to speak wasn't an issue; his willingness to was, though, and his occupational therapist had told us the previous week that we needed to prompt him more often to tell us what he wanted instead of pointing to things and grunting.

Zac looked at me with a glare, and I knew this would be a fight later. That was okay. He was new to dealing with kids on the spectrum. I'd been dealing with one my whole life—me.

"Tell me what that is," I pushed the boy. As I expected, he threw the hotdog and the stick into the fire and stomped over to the chairs we had on the back patio, sitting with his back to us.

Zac pulled the hotdog and stick out of the fire and threw them into the trash before he stomped inside. I looked to the sky and asked the Universe for patience. Suddenly, Dakota jumped up from the chair and ran inside.

I hurried to follow, hoping to keep both of them from getting upset, but when I got inside, I found Dakota with his arms around Zac's waist as they both cried. Zac leaned down and kissed the top of the little boy's head, and I knew in that moment, they'd found each other. "Shh, sweet boy. It's okay. We'll get through this together, the three of us." Those quiet words brought tears to my eyes.

Dakota was going to get mad at one or the other of us, but as long as he knew he had someone to go to for comfort, we'd be okay. I'd only had Mom, and I loved her for being my savior, but I wanted more for Dakota. Now, I knew he had both of us.

Christmastime was busy. Zac and I took Dakota to a few small parties hosted by families who also had kids attending the same occupational therapy group as him, so they were very low key, which was good. He still wore the earmuffs everywhere, and after the first of the year, we were taking him to get his hearing checked to be sure it was normal. I remembered hating it when Mom had taken me, but it was necessary—that didn't mean I looked forward to how upset the boy would be while going through it.

We were spending Christmas Eve at Mom's house so Dakota could be with Melvin, who wasn't getting any better. "If I call you and say to come get him, you will, right? It won't be good for him to see the paramedics or the funeral home take his grandfather away," Mom told me as we set the table for dinner.

"You think it's that close?" I asked her, glancing into the living room where Melvin was sitting in Martin's chair with an oxygen tube under his nose. He was wearing the new pajamas Dakota had picked out for him when Zac took him on a quick shopping trip to Hardy's Dry Goods while I was installing their new cabinets behind the cash register.

Martin came into the kitchen and hugged my mom. "I think I better call that hospice lady. I can tell he's in pain, but he won't say anything because of Dakota."

"Okay." Mom then turned to me. "Can you take all the presents to your house? We'll come by in the morning to open them up. I'll bring breakfast, okay? Will you eat some eggs? I know Dakota loves them, and Zac can definitely put some away. He looks thin, Angus."

I chuckled. "He's been on a diet. He said he's gotten lazy, so he's started snow shoeing on the days you guys have Dakota here for school. I told him he looks good to me, but you know how stubborn he can be."

"How stubborn who can be? Gus? Oh, yeah—just like a mule," Zac said, a mischievous smile on his handsome face. He was carrying his wineglass and Dakota's juice glass, likely coming in for a refill.

"Martin's going to call the hospice lady. Can you keep Dakota occupied while I gather the presents and put them in the truck? We'll take Dakota home with us tonight, and they'll come over in the morning to open gifts," I explained.

Zac turned to Mom, who nodded. "Damn," he sighed before he went into the living room. "Dakota, let's go over to the farm and finish decorating our tree, you wanna?"

We'd put up a tree and Zac had put the lights and ornaments on it, but we hadn't put the tinsel on it. We were planning to do it that night because we thought we'd be hosting Christmas, but Mom had called and said they were afraid to take Melvin out because he wasn't feeling well.

"Pop-pop coming?" Dakota asked, as he pointed toward the living room.

"No, just us, but Santa will come after we go to sleep," Zac offered, holding out his hand for the boy.

"Hang on," I said as I scooped the boy up and walked into the living room with him.

I put him on Melvin's lap and kneeled down in front of the two of them. "How about a picture?" I suggested as I lifted my phone from my pocket.

Melvin whispered, "Take this off me. I don't want him to think of me bein' sick."

I did as he asked, removing the oxygen tube from under his nose and allowing him to situate himself for a picture with his grandson. It was hard for me to see them through my own tears, so I decided a video was better.

I nodded to Melvin, and he smiled at Dakota, who wasn't wearing his earmuffs. "Grandson, I want you to remember how much I love you. You will always be my perfect little boy."

Damn! That reminded me so much of things my mother had said to me over the years that I nearly lost it. Zac's hand was on my shoulder to steady me, and I appreciated it.

Melvin nodded, so I lifted Dakota from his grandfather's lap. "Tell Pop-pop you love him," I said as I held him so he could kiss the old man on the cheek.

"Love you, Pop-pop," he said before I pulled him up and carried him into the kitchen, where Mom helped him get his snowsuit on. Zac and Martin quickly gathered the packages as I helped Melvin pull the oxygen tube over his head and situated the tubing over his ears.

When I turned to walk away, Melvin grabbed my arm. I kneeled down again and stared at him. "I know you'll take care of him. Maybe remind him about me every once in a while. The papers are with the lawyer, Gus. You and Zac will be good dads for him."

"Thank you for picking us, Melvin. We will be sure he grows into a man you'll be proud of," I offered before I stood, leaning down to kiss the man on his wet cheek.

That night, Melvin Standing Bear, a proud member of the Oglala Nation and a loving grandfather, passed away in my parents' home. Mom said he knew Dakota was in excellent hands with us, which was why he felt ready to let go of the pain. For the rest of my life, I'd be grateful to the man who believed I was good enough to take care of the only person he had left on the earth, his grandson.

Chapter Thirteen

Zac

"Plant this one," Dakota directed, as we were putting the seedlings in the patch Gus had made for a garden behind our house.

Monica was helping us—I'd never put in a garden before and I really wondered if I'd ever do it again, but it was in honor of Melvin, who always planted a tiny garden behind his house. It had been Dakota's job to go pick a tomato for their lunch in the summer. We were doing our best to keep alive the traditions Dakota had grown up with when he lived with his grandfather. I was happy to try.

I took the seedling from him and put it into the hole, gently smashing the surrounding dirt around it before we moved to the next hole. The ground had thawed, and Gus had taken the rotary tiller that Martin had left to his grandson to make a garden patch beside the barn.

The two of them had tilled the ground together, Dakota walking in front of Gus with his hands on the handles and the sound-cancelling headphones covering his ears so we had a nice size spot to test our green thumbs. I wasn't sure if I even had one, but with Monica supervising, I felt confident it would turn out..

"What's this called?" I asked Dakota as I took another little plant from him and put it into the dirt.

"Corn," he read from the paper Monica had taped to the front of the tray. We'd been so happy to attend his assessment at the OT center—much like a parent-teacher conference when I was a kid.

I vaguely remembered my mother coming home and telling me I couldn't take her makeup to school anymore and do makeovers on the girls in the class. How she didn't know I was gay back then would forever remain a mystery to me.

What we were happy to learn from the therapist was that Dakota didn't have any learning disabilities. In fact, he was a quick study and could read and write easily—when he was in the mood. I was so proud of him when we left, my buttons were busting.

"Where's 'Ngus?" Dakota asked. He was holding the tray for me while I squatted down to do the planting. We'd been trading off doing it because it was definitely hard on the quads. I needed to go to the shop and start using some of Gus' weights.

"Angus went to dig up a stump. He wants to make us a patio table so we can eat outside when the weather gets warmer like you and Pop-pop Mel used to do," I answered.

We talked about Pop-pop being in heaven with Dakota's grandmother and mother, and Dakota took it better than I'd imagined. I wasn't sure how much he understood about death, but Monica told me we were doing well with allowing him to ask questions instead of pushing information at him that he might not be ready to comprehend.

Sometimes, it was hard to feel as if I was accomplishing anything with Dakota, but I guessed things were okay since he'd agreed to stay at the farm with me when Gus was busy.

"What do you want for lunch?" I asked him as we neared the end of the corn row.

"Grilled cheese and red soup," Dakota responded.

"Tomato soup?" I asked, smiling at his determination that red soup was a good name for tomato soup. He had a point. If anyone said red soup, most of America would know it was tomato soup.

Dakota nodded and gave me a grin that lit up my heart. His big brown eyes showed he was actually happy, which made me ecstatic in return.

The little meltdown he'd suffered last winter before Christmas when we were making hotdogs after our sledding party had opened the floodgates—more or less—for Dakota to talk to us and answer us when we asked him questions.

It was a relief not to have to guess what he wanted and risk another tantrum if I misinterpreted his wishes while we were roasting hot dogs. I thought Gus was being mean when he pushed Dakota to tell him what condiment he wanted on his bun, but I should have known better.

My Gus was coming at the situation from a place of experience, having lived with autism his whole life. He knew what to do in that instant, and I had to admit I was at a disadvantage.

Later that night, after we took Dakota back to Martin and Monica's house—Mel was still alive back then—Gus and I had a serious discussion. I knew my man was wise, but he reminded me just how much without rubbing my nose in it.

"Are you done being mad at me?" my handsome woodsman asked as he drove us back to the farm.

"I knew what he wanted, Gus. He didn't need to say exactly what it was," I snapped at him. I believed he'd been hard on Dakota to the point the boy became upset, and I was pissed about it.

Later, Gus and I were stripping off for bed, and when I went to the dresser and pulled out a pair of pajama pants and a t-shirt, he let go with a loud groan. Pajamas meant no nookie, and Gus never liked the idea he couldn't sweet talk me into making love. I was too angry at him to even think about it.

"What would you think if you were in the grocery store and a grown man stood in the aisle, pointed to the mustard, and said 'This?' Would you think there was something wrong with him?" Gus asked, but it sounded like Monica's words coming out of his mouth.

I was about to give him a witty retort as the visual formed in my mind's eye. Suddenly, I understood what he meant. He didn't want Dakota to be the subject of ridicule, and while he was young, it was necessary to help him learn things so he could thrive. I finally got Gus' motivation. It was humbling.

That was a hard lesson for *me* to learn, but I did, and as I took over driving Dakota to OT, I paid more attention to the therapists and the skills they taught so I could help reinforce them at home the way Gus did.

After the last corn stalk seedling was in the ground, Dakota helped me clean up the trays to return to Monica. "Wanna walk down to the mailbox with me?" I asked him as George appeared from nowhere. Gus was working in the shop, so I was assuming Gus had let him out for a little while.

Dakota picked up George, who purred like the happy tomcat he was, and the three of us walked down to the mailbox. We stopped at the end of the driveway, and Dakota pulled open the handle, allowing me to reach inside for the mail.

"You wanna make up a story like Gus tells? Let's think of one about a cat," I suggested. Dakota had started telling me stories like the ones Gus told him, and sometimes they were even the same ones Gus told with subtle changes. It was truly sweet and reinforced for me that Gus' stories needed to be available to a much wider audience than just Dakota and me.

I found an official envelope in the stack addressed to Gus and me, so I put the rest of the junk under my arm as Dakota told me a story about a cat named George.

I listened as I opened the thick envelope, pulling out a fistful of papers. It was a hearing notice for the fifth of May in Tyndall at the Bon Homme County Court House. "Notice to Appear in the Matter of Guardianship of Dakota Standing Bear," was the title of the paper, and my heart leaped into my throat.

When Melvin's estate was settled back in January, Gus and I had been granted temporary guardianship of Dakota. It was surprising the time had gone by so quickly, but suddenly, the nerves were back in full force.

I folded the papers and stuffed them back into the envelope, turning to give Dakota my complete attention. I wondered if I was ready until I heard... "Ow, George. You scratch. It's okay."

I glanced down to see that George wanted down, and he'd scratched Dakota's forearm, and when Dakota let go of the cat, he stepped closer to me and took my hand. "Look," he said, drawing my attention to the three little lines where George had left his mark.

"Oh, I'm sorry. I don't think he meant to hurt you. Let's go inside and put some medicine on it and one of those Animal strips on it," I suggested, referring to the Muppets bandages we'd bought at the store. Animal, the red drummer puppet with the unibrow, was Dakota's favorite.

"He didn't mean it," Dakota told me with so much compassion in his voice for the cat as we hurried to the house that I had tears in my eyes. I really needed to talk to Gus about the papers and what they meant. It was definitely time for the serious discussion about our future.

Chapter Fourteen

Gus

"Lunch!" I heard as there was a tug on my jeans. I turned off the sander and took off the industrial noise-canceling safety headphones I used in the shop, which were like the smaller set I had for Dakota. When I turned around, I was happy to see he'd put his pair on when he came into the shop, just as I'd taught him when I was working with machinery.

His pair was red—his favorite color—and they hung right inside the door of the workshop on a nail that was easy for him to reach. He had a grin on his face and that always made me happy. He and Zac had been working in the little garden we were planting, and I'd seen the two of them walking down to the mailbox earlier.

I took off my headphones and placed them on the workbench, reaching down to pick him up and put him on the stool I'd made for him. I handed him the hand broom as he kneeled on the wide seat. "You wanna clean off the sawdust for me?" I asked him as I stood behind him so he didn't fall off.

"Yep," he answered before he began sweeping the sawdust into the center of the piece I was making, just as I'd shown him. I grabbed the accompanying dustpan and held it under the large piece of mahogany for Dakota to sweep the sawdust into. It was a ritual the two of us shared, and I enjoyed it as much as he did.

"Look," Dakota told me as he held out his little arm. There were two Muppet bandages on his arm.

I leaned forward and put a kiss on them before I looked at him. "What happened, Kota?"

I fell in love with Zac fast, but I knew it was right when I got to know him. I couldn't believe I had grown to love the little boy almost as fast, but it made sense.

"George scratched me," he answered with his bottom lip sticking out.

"Sweetheart, are you ready for lunch?" Zac asked from the door of the workshop.

I took Dakota off the stool and held his hand as we walked over to the door where Zac was leaning. I kissed his lips, feeling all my love for him. He was the perfect one for me, and now I had another perfect person in my life. I was lucky.

"What are we having?" I asked as I picked Zac up and tossed him over my shoulder, happy to hear Dakota's laugh.

"What are we having, Dakota?" Zac asked as he pinched my butt while we walked to the house.

"Grilled cheese and red soup," Dakota announced with a laugh in his voice. It was a fantastic day.

We went into the house and Zac sent the two of us to wash up while he finished our sandwiches. Zac liked cheddar-jalapeño cheese. Kota liked American cheese, and I liked a combo of both. I also liked pickled jalapeno peppers on mine, and Zac knew exactly how to grill it so it was just right. It was thick and delicious with the extra cheese, but if somebody was eating a grilled cheese, it should be gooey and satisfying.

After the table was set, Zac got the three of us some lemonade and sat down across from Kota. "Did you tell 'Ngus the story about George scratching you?"

I turned to Kota and waited for him to tell me—in detail—what had happened. He loved to tell us stories, as much as I'd loved to tell them when I was younger. Most of them were from his imagination, but I believed his stories showed he was smart and creative.

Dakota loved to read to me from my old stories at night before he went to bed, and sometimes he added to them, which made me smile. I needed to have Zac sit and write Dakota's retelling of them down so we would always have them. That way, it would be a family thing, not just a *Gus* thing.

"Oh, he didn't mean to do it. He got excited because he saw a deer in the woods, I bet," Dakota explained between tiny bites of his sandwich. He reminded me of a little squirrel the way he ate, but I didn't tease him. He looked really cute.

"Okay. Maybe he'll tell you he's sorry when we put him in the shed later. How are you, my love?" I asked Zac.

"I sent off a draft of your story and jpegs of the drawings you and Dakota made to go with 'Mike and Me.' We'll see what happens," Zac said.

I nodded as Zac grabbed an envelope from the chair next to him, a big smile on his face as he laid it next to my plate.

I picked up my napkin and wiped my fingers of the buttery goodness before grabbing the envelope and pulling out the papers to see a lot more stuff than I wanted to read. "It looks like court stuff," I offered as I read the title of the first page. *Notice to Appear...*

I glanced at Zac and shrugged. His face scrunched into the impatient expression he gave me when I wasn't really paying attention to him. "It's a notice that the court is ready to decide about custody," he answered, twitching his head in Dakota's direction.

"Oh... *Oh!*" I was stunned for a second, but my dream was about to come true.

Later that day after Kota and I closed up the shop and made sure George was inside since the temperature was going to be near freezing that night, the three of us watched a movie together before we put Dakota to bed in the old twin he had from Melvin's house.

The tutor was coming in the morning. If he didn't get enough rest, Dakota would be difficult for her to teach anything.

Kota read us a chapter from a mystery book written for kids on the spectrum that the three of us were enjoying, and then Zac kissed his forehead goodnight, leaving the two of us to talk a little before bed.

"Your arm okay?" I asked as I tucked Kota into the quilt he had that was made by his grandmother. We'd brought it with his things from Melvin's house, and it made him feel safe.

Melvin's house had been a two-bedroom rental. He'd moved from his family home on the Pine Ridge Conservation after his daughter left home and his wife died, deciding to settle in Scotland to be closer to work, and that was where he'd met Martin years ago.

Emptying the rental had been sad, but Mom had watched Dakota while Martin, Zac, and I had cleaned out the house. The man's belongings had been left to Dakota, along with a small life insurance policy through the Plumber's Union that we'd put into a savings account for the future. The furniture and knick-knacks were stored in the barn loft for Dakota to go through when he was older and ready.

"George is very sorry for hurting me. He ran after the deer to keep it away from our garden," Dakota told me. He was so serious that it made me chuckle.

"Oh, good! He's doing his job, then, isn't he? That's what we need," I said as I turned on the nightlight. I made sure he was settled before I sat forward and whispered to him.

"Do you think you'd like it if Zac and I were your parents? You know how Martin and Monica are my parents? Do you want to be part of Zac's and my family?" I asked, feeling nerves flare in my stomach.

Dakota stared at me for a few seconds with his gigantic brown eyes before he nodded, which helped me relax.

"Okay. So, we'll go meet a judge, and we can see about making sure things are permanent. You think about it for a few days, and if you're not sure, that's fine. You can tell me or Zac or Monica how you feel about it, and we'll figure things out from there, okay?"

Dakota nodded, and I leaned forward and kissed his forehead, hoping he *did* decide he wanted us for his parents. I couldn't force him to do something he didn't want to do, and I knew Zac would be upset if he didn't want us, but I was sure we would survive as long as we had each other. We had a lot of love to guide us. We'd be disappointed, but we still had each other.

I stopped in the hall bathroom and turned on the small nightlight in case Dakota needed to go through the night. We were so glad he'd stopped wetting the bed because he'd adjusted to our farmhouse. That had been an anxious time for all of us.

I was making him a new headboard and footboard in the wood shop. Zac had ordered a new bed frame, mattress, and box springs once the bedwetting had stopped, and I wanted him to love it. I planned to carve his name on the headboard with baby animals around it.

I had finished the chicken coop I'd been building before Christmas, but I hadn't told Zac about it yet. He thought it was another thing I got a whim to do, but I wanted us to have some laying hens, and I thought having some chicks running around might make Dakota happy.

I'd cut a large hole in the barn's north wall to bring them inside where it was heated in the winter, and Martin was going to help me install automatic water coolers inside and outside. It was going to be top of the line, all the way.

I made my way back to the bedroom, stopping to check the thermostat like I always remembered Martin doing after Mom and I came to live with him. I wasn't sure why he did it back then, but now I knew it was because he wanted to make sure his family was comfortable at night. He loved us, and that was a way he showed it.

I stepped into our bedroom to find Zac leaning against the headboard with his laptop. He wasn't wearing a shirt... *Yes!*

"Let me take a quick shower. Don't move an inch," I told him.

He giggled in response, which made me smile.

I hurried through my routine to get back to bed before he changed his mind, and when I opened the bathroom door, Zac was on top of the covers with his hard dick in his hand, and a bottle of lube on the quilt next to him.

I clicked the lock on the bedroom door and jumped on the bed, leaning down to lick the head of his cock. His moan of pleasure was a song to me.

I had to kiss him the whole time we made love because he could be loud and now we had another person living with us. Plus, I loved the contact of our tongues swirling together. The moans and groans he made vibrated through my body, too, and the high-pitched little squeak he made just before he shot off all pleased me beyond words.

I'd put our king-sized bed on gripping coasters because we had wooden floors—that I'd put down myself—and the bed tended to slide around because we got up to it pretty good when we had sex. I'd had to patch the wall after our first anniversary before Kota came into our lives. That was a good night.

After I cleaned us both up, I unlocked the door and cracked it in case we were needed. I slid on boxer briefs while my Zac pulled on pretty pink panties before we settled in for sleep. The sight of him in them got me going again, but we had an early morning the next day.

"I love you," I whispered into his ear after he burrowed into my body like always—unless he was mad. But even those nights, he ended up finding me in his sleep. We were meant to be.

Chapter Fifteen

Zac

"Both of you stop fidgeting with your necks. It'll only be about fifteen minutes," I hissed at Gus and Dakota. We were in the back of the courtroom at the Bon Homme County Courthouse, and we were waiting for our turn with the judge. It was family court day because the courthouse wasn't big enough to have more than one courtroom, so certain cases were heard on certain days.

My boys were wearing ties that neither of them wanted to leave alone. Gus' was borrowed from Martin. It was a bolo style with a turquoise pendant. It looked so striking on him that I nearly jumped him before we left the house.

Dakota was wearing one that had been Melvin's. The leather strings were a little long on him, but the beautiful pendant was made from polished silver, with a golden bear standing on its back legs. It fit that Melvin should be there to give his blessing to us as we became Dakota's parents.

I hoped he was looking down on us with that big grin I remembered seeing every time he looked at his grandson. It hadn't been easy to adjust to having Dakota with us. I'd been scared and overjoyed in equal measure as we all learned to become a family.

I had certainly learned a lesson in gratitude that Melvin had decided that Gus and I should take Dakota to be our son. I knew we'd do everything in our power to live up to the man's expectations for seeing that his grandson reached his potential.

I chuckled as I watched Gus fidgeting with the neck of his shirt. He slid the pendant down a bit each time, and he had just unbuttoned the top button when I grabbed his hand and squeezed it. "Only a few more minutes, I'm sure."

Just then, our attorney, Joshua Bauer, came into the courtroom and slid into the seat next to Gus. "You guys ready? Judge Caster enjoys handling cases like yours. He's always happy to have a new family created in his courtroom."

I leaned around Dakota, who was between us, and looked at Joshua. "Even if the parents are both dads?"

Josh offered a knowing smile. "I dated his son while I was in law school. He's not your typical jurist. No worries."

Twenty minutes later, the four of us were standing in front of the bench, Dakota wearing his earmuffs, which Josh had already cleared with the clerk after explaining that he was on the autism spectrum.

"Are we okay to proceed?" the judge asked Josh.

"Yes, your honor, and thank you for not banging the gavel. My client has sensitive hearing," Josh said.

The judge smirked as he pushed up his glasses and looked at the three of us. Dakota shrunk behind Gus a little, but he didn't let go of my hand. "I'll make this quick, gentlemen. Is it your desire..."

Ten minutes later, Monica and Martin were taking pictures of us with the judge, and it was confirmed that we would be the guardians of Dakota Standing Bear. We hadn't asked for adoption to keep from having to appear before the tribal court, and we wouldn't be changing Dakota's surname. In every other aspect, Dakota Standing Bear was our little boy.

We left the courthouse and went to Monica's for lunch, skipping a restaurant meal because of the noise. The second we got out of the truck, both Gus and Dakota took off their ties, which made me laugh. I slipped off my own and put it in the pocket of my suit jacket, happy I didn't have to wear them to work any longer.

All of us hurried inside to see Monica had decorated the house with pictures of balloons and a big "Welcome to the Family" sign. As Monica was taking more pictures of Dakota in front of the sign, my phone rang.

I looked at the number, seeing a New York area code, so I answered. "Zachary Foxx McMurray."

"Zeke! It's Penelope Prentiss. Shame on you for sending that story to my sister. Thankfully, I intercepted it from her inbox. She's out on maternity leave at the moment. Anyway, what's new with you?"

"I just became a father—"

"That's lovely. So, this story? This is from the man I sent you out to recruit in South Dakota when you worked for me?" Penelope asked, the usual self-important tone in her voice that I remembered far too well.

"The man who is my husband now? Yes," I answered, looking into the kitchen to see Gus kneeling on the floor next to Dakota, the two of them making funny faces as Monica snapped pictures of them and Martin laughed. My heart was overflowing.

"Good on you, Zeke. Anyway, who did your illustrations? They're a little primitive. We'll want to get professional illustrations done," she stated.

I had to stop her right there. She wasn't my boss any longer, and she wasn't going to roll over me as she'd done in the past. "No. Our son drew those illustrations, and those are the ones Angus wants to use. If you don't like them, then we can't do business, I'm afraid. Oh—and I've already filed the copyrights on all the stories, so no going around me."

There was silence for a moment, and then I heard a cackle through the line. "Joy? Is that you?" Penelope snapped.

There was another loud laugh, which made me smile, and then my old friend Joy spoke up. "Good for you, Zachary. Congratulations on all of your accomplishments. If she doesn't do right by you, call me. I know many people in the business." There was a click on the other end and then silence.

"I should have fired that old cow years ago. What are your terms?" Penelope asked.

I looked at Gus and Dakota, who were setting the table, and I grinned. "Penny, darling, I'll have to call you back. We're celebrating a family milestone."

I hung up and joined the party. There was always time to worry about business, but Dakota would only become our son once.

That evening when we got home from Monica and Martin's house, Gus went to the workshop and came back with his tool pouch and his headphones, along with Dakota's. "What are you guys going to do?" I asked.

It was still light outside, so I followed Gus and Dakota to the front yard. Gus picked up the tree stump where the top had been carved into a book, and he reached into the pocket of his khaki slacks, pulling out a black magic marker and handing it to Dakota.

"Write your name there," he said as he pointed to a spot on the book just below the carving of our wedding rings and the date of our wedding.

Dakota did as Gus asked, and then my woodsman slid on his safety goggles and went to work. Dakota came to sit with me on the porch in the beautiful rocking chairs that Gus had made for us, and the two of us watched.

"What's he doin'?" Dakota asked.

I smiled, fighting the tears that wanted to flow so quickly. "He's carving you into our family album. You're our son, and we're your dads now. That book shows all the important days in our lives—even George is in there. Angus made it after we got married, and now you're in the book forever," I said, my voice cracking.

Dakota grinned. "I'm in the book."

Epilogue

♥

Angus McMurray

Ten years later...

"I see him," Zac announced as the two of us stood on the bleachers in the gym of Scotland Senior High School. It wasn't huge, but then again, the town we called home wasn't enormous.

"Oh, he looks so handsome," Mom gushed behind us. She and Martin were there like always, supporting our family in the next chapter of our lives.

Dakota was graduating from high school. It was a day we'd always hoped we'd see, and now here we were. I knew in my heart that Kota could do it, though sometimes, it seemed we might not make it, but here we were... and our son was graduating in the top three of his class. We were so proud of him, and we couldn't wait to see what was next.

Our son and I had become small-town celebrities in Scotland. The stories I wrote all those years ago had been published through Prentiss & Pollard, the publishing company where Zac had worked for a brief time many years ago.

Dakota had added to the stories with details only he saw as he looked at the world, and he'd drawn all the illustrations for the ten-book series. The series had won awards because its main character was a young boy who was on the autism spectrum, and we'd just been informed it was going to be made into a cartoon series for public television.

The money we'd made from selling the series to a production company was sending our boy to a design school in Vancouver, and Zac and I were scared to death to let him go alone, but Kota had asked to try. Like my husband repeated to me all the time—*it was only a plane ride away.*

The progress Dakota had made since becoming a member of our family had been incredible. His earmuffs had been replaced with wireless ear buds because he was still sensitive to sounds, but he was self-sufficient and had a thirst for learning everything he could that we didn't want to hinder in any way—or so I'd been told by my mother and my husband.

I had a lot of gray in my blond hair now. Zac had taught Dakota to drive my old stick-shift Ford, which made me laugh. I'd traded it in for the Chevy I was still driving, but Zac had Martin take him to Sioux Falls to buy it back.

Martin had a friend of his rebuild the engine, and Zac paid for it with his freelance jobs. It had been my birthday present when I turned forty, and I'd been very surprised.

Martin also taught Zac to drive a stick, which was why he taught Kota to drive it. Both of my boys were amazing and filled me with joy every day.

"Oh, he's going up to give his speech. He looks calm, right?" Zac whispered as Kota walked on the stage with the faculty and administration, taking a seat next to the principal.

I saw Dakota reach up after the applause died down, and I noticed him slip the earbuds into the pocket of his slacks. I knew the next part would be hard for him, but I had faith in him—he'd come so far from the little boy we'd met ten years ago. He'd grown into a fine young man. I was proud of him, and I knew his family in heaven must be as well.

I wasn't much of a religious man, but I believed there was something bigger than all of us that helped guide us on our path. My path led me to a beautiful man who wanted to publish my stories that I'd written when I was a kid. In the end, he'd gotten what he wanted, and I was part of that bargain.

I never looked back at anything that happened in our lives with regret. Every misstep, regardless of how minor it might be, led Zachary Foxx to me and me to him.

That higher power brought a little boy—with challenges much like my own—into our lives when we were ready for him. Learning how to help him become the man sitting on that stage had been as much a gift to us as I'd ever imagined I'd get.

The ten-year-old boy that Monica McMurray had met at that group home hadn't known how to cope with the world around him. He'd been abused and abandoned, but with love and lots of patience, he'd built a good business. He'd met a wonderful man and fallen in love, lucky to get that man to marry him, and now, he'd raised a son who was about to give the graduation address at his high school.

I'd say my life wasn't just perfect... It was 2perfect.

Zac

A nudge against my shoulder caught my attention as I listened to the principal talk about the graduating class. I glanced up to see Joy, Penelope's assistant, standing in front of me with a smile.

I scooted everyone down and allowed her a seat next to me. "What are you doing here?" I whispered.

Joy smiled and touched my arm. "I wouldn't miss this for the world. I can't believe how much he's grown, Zac. I'm as proud of him as if he were my grandson."

Over the years that we'd been working with P&P to publish Gus' stories with Dakota's illustrations, Joy and Dakota had become friends. She'd sit with him in the break room while I fought with Penelope over edits she wanted to make to the manuscript, and Gus would pace in frustration. *Fun times!*

Now, here we were at Dakota's graduation before he went off to design school. There was money from the book and public television deals, along with what Melvin had left him, and it would more than pay his tuition and set him up with a place to live and incidentals he might need while he was in school.

Gus' old Ford, which had been completely refurbished, would take him and all of his things up to Vancouver. I was worried, nervous, proud, and excited for our son. It was a huge, scary new adventure for him—and us—but as his parents, we knew he needed the chance to try.

"It is my pleasure to introduce Dakota Standing Bear to deliver the graduation address," the principal announced.

Gus grabbed my hand, and the two of us held our breath as Dakota stood and walked to the podium.

"Thank you, Principal Marcus. Members of the administration, faculty, parents, and fellow students, I'm Dakota Standing Bear McMurray, and I'm proud to be giving the graduation address. I'm not at the top of the class, but my fellow students voted for me to share my journey, so here I go."

Dakota opened the notebook he'd carried with him, and I crossed the fingers of my right hand. He'd worked so hard on the speech, and I could hear the nerves in his voice.

The gym was quiet as a church as Dakota crafted his tale, just as he'd done since he'd come to live with us. Monica reached over my shoulder and handed me a pack of tissues as I listened to him telling the story of living with autism and all the hurdles he'd had to jump while he was growing up.

How things others took for granted were major challenges for him, and how much his occupational therapists and his tutors from grade school had helped him learn and grow. Gus reached for the tissue pack I held in my hand and took one, handing it to Anders Milton, who was sitting on the other side of him, who then handed it to my best friend, Luke Ladeaux Milton. Theirs was a story to tell another time.

I had a steady stream of tears flowing down my face, but Gus just sat next to me with a big grin. That was—until Dakota started talking about his fathers and grandparents.

"I had a rough start, but I had many people in my future I couldn't have imagined. My grandfather, Melvin Standing Bear, was my rock, but unfortunately, he died when I was eight. He made it his mission before he left this earth to find a family who would love me, take care of me, and, most importantly, understand me. He chose right. My grandmother, Monica, my grandfather, Martin, and my dads, Angus and Zachary. They all gave me more love and support than I ever knew I would need."

I glanced at Gus to see the tears, and I squeezed his hand and offered him a tissue. I knew he couldn't sit through that entire speech and not cry, the big softie.

As Dakota's remarks were ending, I smiled as he reached into his pocket and retrieved his earbuds, covertly sliding them into his ears before he said, "Congratulations to all of us. We have accomplished a lot, and I know we're excited to see what's waiting for us on this path called life."

He closed his notebook and took a seat as the place erupted in applause. Gus and I stood with all the other people in the gym, and Gus hugged me.

“Perfect.”

Yep, that summed it up.

About Sam E. Kraemer/ L.A. Kaye

♥

Sam E. Kraemer
AUTHOR OF MM ROMANCE

I grew up in the rural Midwest before moving to the East Coast with a dashing young man who swept me off my feet. We've now settled in the desert Southwest where I write M/M contemporary romance. I also write paranormal M/M romance under "Sam E. Kraemer writing as L. A. Kaye." I'm a firm believer that love is love, regardless of how it presents itself, and I'm proud to be a staunch ally of the LGBTQIA+ community. I have a loving, supportive family, and I feel blessed by the universe and thankful every day for all I have been given. In my heart and soul, I believe I hit the cosmic jackpot.

Cheers!

Other Books by Sam E. Kraemer/ L.A. Kaye

♥

Books by Sam E. Kraemer

The Lonely Heroes Complete Series

Ranger Hank

Guardian Gabe

Cowboy Shep

Hacker Lawry

Positive Raleigh

Salesman Mateo

Bachelor Hero

Orphan Duke

Noble Bruno

Avenging Kelly

Chef Rafe

Baby Romeo

On The Rocks Complete Series

Whiskey Dreams

Ima-GIN-ation

Absinthe Minded

Weighting... Complete Series

Weighting...Box Set

Weighting for Love

Weighting for Laughter

Weighting for a Lifetime

May/December Hearts Collection

A Wise Heart

Heart of Stone

What the H(e)art Wants

A Flaws & All Love Story

Sinners' Redemption

Forgiveness is a Virtue

Swim Coach

Love & Cowboys

Love & Cowboys Box Set

For the Love of the Bull Rider

For the Love of the Lawyer

For the Love of the Broken Man

Luv by Numbers Series

Sums of the Heart

Subtracting the Heart

Greater than the Heart

Prey for the Hunter

When Sparks Fly

Givin' Me Fitz

Men of Memphis Blues

Kim & Skip

Cash & Cary

Dori & Sonny

Perfect Novellas

Perfect

2 Perfect

Power Players

The Senator

Holiday Books

My Jingle Bell Heart

Georgie's Eggcellent Adventure

The Holiday Gamble

Mabry's Minor Mistake

Sheer Bliss Holiday

Kiss Me Stupid

A Daddy for Christmas 2: Hermie

A Little Christmas 4: Teller

Other Titles

Unbreak Him

The Secrets We Whisper To The Bees

Shear Bliss

Foggy Basin Season 1

Smolder

The Road to Rocktoberfest 2024

Accidental Fire

The Road to Rocktoberfest 2025

Lost Little Boy

Pride Summer Camp 2025

BOOKS by L.A. Kaye

Dearly and The Departed

Dearly & Deviant Daniel

Dearly & Vain Valentino

Dearly & Notorious Nancy

Dearly & Homeless Horace

Dearly& Threatening Thane

Dearly & Lovesick Lorraine

Dearly and The Departed Spinoffs

The Harbinger's Ball

The Harbinger's Allure

Scotty & Jay's First Hellish Adventure

Scotty & Jay's Second Hellish Adventure

Other Titles

Halston's Family Gothic - The Prologue

The Mysteries of Marblehead Manor

Mutual Obsessions

9 798224 289097

Printed by Libri Plureos GmbH in Hamburg,
Germany